"Tell me you want me."

"I want you, but there's—" Emily stepped back from Loukas with what little willpower she had left, but she stumbled over the pedal bin behind her left foot and it tipped over and spilled its contents in front of his Italian leather–clad feet.

An unpinned grenade would have had a similar effect.

Loukas's face drained of color like he was the one with morning sickness. He stood frozen for a moment. Totally statue-like, as if someone had pressed a pause button on him.

Emily watched as if in slow motion when he bent to pick up not one but seven test wands. He examined the telltale blue lines, the wands clanking against each other like chopsticks. His eyes finally cut to hers, sharp, flint-hard with query. "You're...*pregnant*?"

One Night With Consequences

When one night...leads to pregnancy!

When succumbing to a night of unbridled desire
it's impossible to think past the morning after!

But, with the sheets barely settled, that little blue line
appears on the pregnancy test and it doesn't take
long to realize that one night of white-hot passion
has turned into a lifetime of consequences!

Only one question remains:

How do you tell a man you've just met that you're
about to share more than just his bed?

Find out in:

Look for more **One Night With Consequences** stories
coming soon!

Melanie Milburne

A RING FOR THE GREEK'S BABY

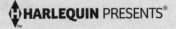

HARLEQUIN PRESENTS®

Recycling programs
for this product may
not exist in your area.

ISBN-13: 978-0-373-06091-7

A Ring for the Greek's Baby

First North American Publication 2017

Copyright © 2017 by Melanie Milburne

Printed in U.S.A.

www.Harlequin.com

Melanie Milburne read her first Harlequin novel at the age of seventeen, in between studying for her final exams. After completing a master's degree in education she decided to write a novel, and thus her career as a romance author was born. Melanie is an ambassador for the Australian Childhood Foundation and a keen dog lover and trainer. She enjoys long walks in the Tasmanian bush. In 2015 Melanie won the HOLT Medallion—a prestigious award honoring outstanding literary talent.

Books by Melanie Milburne

Harlequin Presents

The Temporary Mrs. Marchetti
Unwrapping His Convenient Fiancée
His Mistress for a Week
At No Man's Command
His Final Bargain

Wedlocked!

Wedding Night with Her Enemy

The Ravensdale Scandals

Ravensdale's Defiant Captive
Awakening the Ravensdale Heiress
Engaged to Her Ravensdale Enemy
The Most Scandalous Ravensdale

The Chatsfield

Playboy's Lesson
Chatsfield's Ultimate Acquisition

The Playboys of Argentina

The Valquez Bride
The Valquez Seduction

Visit the Author Profile page at Harlequin.com for more titles.

To my darling father, Gordon Luke, who passed away during the writing of this novel. You were an amazing father, grandfather and great-grandfather, brother, uncle and friend. You have touched so many lives with your funny stories, your generous spirit and strong work ethic. I will always treasure the memories I have of our relationship. The world would be a better place if everyone could have a dad like you. Rest in peace. xxx

CHAPTER ONE

WHEN THE SEVENTH TEST came back positive, Emily knew it was time to face the truth. Face it or spend a fortune on pregnancy tests until there wasn't a pharmacy she could walk into in the whole of London without blushing with an 'it's me again' grimace. She'd thought buying a jumbo box of tampons was embarrassing, but a basket full of pregnancy tests was way worse. There was no avoiding it. Those little blue lines weren't lying even if she wished they were.

She. Was. Pregnant.

Not that she didn't want to have a baby. Some day, with some nice guy who was madly in love with her and had married her at a big, white wedding first.

Her first ever one-night stand and look what had happened. How could she be so fertile? How could condoms be so unreliable? How could she have slept with a man so out of her league? Emily was all for aiming high in life, but a Greek billionaire? And not one of those short, fat, balding middle-aged ones, like those in her local deli, but a six-foot-four heart-stoppingly gorgeous man who had eyes so brown you could lose yourself in them.

Which she had promptly done. Completely and utterly lost herself in a sizzling sexual encounter unlike anything she'd experienced before. Which, truth be told, was not saying much, because her experience could hardly be described as extensive given she'd wasted seven years with her ex-partner Daniel. Seven years. *Argh!* Why couldn't the number seven be lucky for her like everyone else? For seven long years she'd waited for a proposal. It had got so bad that every time her ex had bent down on one knee to pick something up off the floor she would get all excited thinking this was it—the moment she'd been waiting for.

It had never happened.

What had happened instead was she'd got cheated on. The ignominy of being betrayed was bad enough, but to be left for a male lover was a whole new level of humiliation. How could she have been the last to know Daniel was gay?

But it wasn't the betrayal that hurt her the most. It was the loss of being a part of a couple; the shock of being single for the first time in so long she had forgotten *how* to be single. Going out at night without a partner by her side felt weird, like going out with only one shoe on. Or eating in a restaurant on her own, working her way through a meal, wondering if everyone was speculating if she'd been stood up or something.

She used to love going out to dinner with Daniel, who was a bit of a food and wine connoisseur. They would try different restaurants and cuisines and sit for hours over a meal, discussing the food, the presentation, the wine and even the other diners. She used to love coming home from work knowing she had someone to talk to about her day. Daniel had been her 'guess what happened to me today' person, her sounding board, her back-up, her anchor. The person who'd provided the stability she'd craved since she was a child.

She hadn't had much luck since with dating. Her New Age relationship-therapist mother said it was because she was subconsciously sabotaging her male relationships because of her father issues. Father issues. And whose fault was it she didn't have a father? Her mother hadn't managed to get his name and number when she'd had sex with him under a rain-soaked tarpaulin at a music festival.

Emily looked at the pregnancy test again. No.

She wasn't having a nightmare. Well, she was. A *living* nightmare. A nightmare that involved fronting up to commitment-phobe Loukas Kyprianos and telling him he was going to be a father.

Oh, joy.

Such a task would be a whole lot easier if he had called her in the month since their night of bed-wrecking, pulse-throbbing sex. Or sent a text message. Or an email. A carrier pigeon, even. Given her some tiny thread of hope he might want to see her again.

Although, come to think of it, she hadn't exactly done herself any favours in that department. She could write a book on how to get a guy to lose interest in one date. When she was nervous she talked too much. Way too much. When she gushed like that, she didn't just wear her heart on her sleeve but on every visible part of her body. A couple of drinks down and she'd mentioned her dream of marriage, four kids and a dog—an Irish Retriever, no less. To a man who had a reputation as an easy come, easy go playboy.

What was *wrong* with her?

Emily walked out of the bathroom and picked up her phone. No missed calls. No text messages… apart from four from her mother with links to her prescribed daily meditation and yoga practices. It was easier to let her mother think she used the links than to argue why she didn't. She had learned a long time ago that arguing with her mother was a pointless and energy draining exercise.

Emily didn't have Loukas's number even if she could summon up the courage to call it. She could get it from her friend Allegra, who was married to Loukas's best friend, Draco Papandreou, but somehow telling Loukas over the phone didn't seem quite the way to go. *Hey, guess what? We made a baby!* would probably not be such a great opening gambit.

No. This called for a face-to-face conversation. She needed to gauge his reaction. Not that he was an easy person to read. He had one of those faces that gave little away in terms of expression. His facial muscles were into energy saving or something. It was like trying to see what was behind a curtained stage. But he had an aura of quiet authority she'd found overwhelmingly attractive. His aloofness had intrigued her at the wedding. He didn't seem to need people the way she did. She was like a too-friendly puppy at a garden party, moving from group to group, trying to win approval.

He, on the other hand, was like a statue.

Emily's phone rang and she almost dropped it in surprise. She didn't recognise the number and answered it in her best legal secretary voice. 'Emily Seymour speaking.'

'It's Loukas Kyprianos.'

Her heart kicked her ribcage out of the way, leapt to her throat and clung there with hooked claws.

He'd called her. He'd called her. He'd called her.

The words were beating in time with her panicked pulse. She needed more time. She wasn't ready for this conversation. She needed to rehearse in front of the mirror or something, like she used to do as a kid with a hairbrush as a pretend microphone. She tried to calm herself but her breathing was so choppy it felt as though she was having an asthma attack.

Breathe. Breathe. Breathe.

She could do with some of her mother's mindfulness techniques right about now. 'Erm…hi. How are you?'

'Fine. You?'

'Erm…good, thank you. Great. Super. Fantastic.'

Apart from a little morning sickness.

There was a tick-tock of silence.

'Are you free this evening?'

Emily swallowed. Free for what? Hook-up sex? She didn't want to sound too available. A girl had her pride and all that. But she had to tell him about the baby. Maybe over dinner would be the best way to do it. No. No. No. Not in a public place. She would have to do it in private. Private was best. 'I'll have to check my diary. I seem to remember I have something…'

He gave a soft sound that could have passed for an amused chuckle. 'You don't have to play hard to get with me, Emily.'

Yes, well, it was a little late for that, she had to admit. The way he said her name with that subtle Greek accent made the base of her spine go all squishy. *Em-il-ee.* It wasn't a name when he said it. It was a seductive caress, as if he had circled each and every bump of her vertebrae with a slow-moving fingertip. 'Look, I think you should know, I'm not usually like that…like I was the night of the wedding. I don't normally drink so much—'

'Have dinner with me.'

Emily took umbrage at the way he said it, like a command instead of an invitation. Did he think she'd been sitting by her phone waiting for him to call? Well, she had, but that was beside the point. She wasn't going to let him think he could call her out of the blue and get her to drop everything to have dinner with him—even if she had nothing to drop. 'I'm not free this evening so—'

'Cancel.'

Cancel?

What the hell? Why should she cancel something at his say-so? 'I don't think so.'

She was quite proud of the haughty I-haven't-been-Superglued-to-my-phone-waiting-for-you-to-call tone in her voice.

'Please?'

Emily let a small silence pass. Let him sweat it out, as she'd been doing for the last month.

'Why do you want to have dinner with me?' she finally asked.

'I want to see you again.' His voice was rough and smooth. Gravel dipped in honey.

He wanted to see her again? Why? He had a reputation as a playboy, perhaps not as wild and loose-living as some rich men, but he hadn't had a relationship lasting longer than a few days.

Or, at least, none the press knew about. Since his best friend's marriage, the media interest had shifted from Draco to Loukas. Before that, Loukas had been able to fly below the radar but now everyone was speculating on whom he would date next. Emily privately had been dreading seeing him with another woman in the weeks since the wedding. If he were involved with someone else then the task of telling him he was to be a father would be even more difficult.

'Is that code for "sleeping with me"?' she asked. 'Because, if so, I think you should know I'm not that sort of girl. I've never had a one-night stand before and I—'

'It wouldn't be a one-night stand if we did it again.'

It was a good point. But she couldn't sleep with him before she told him the result of their last encounter. Even thinking about that night in his arms made her insides do cartwheels of excitement. Listening to his voice was as good as foreplay. If he kept talking to her, who knew what might happen? 'Just dinner, okay?'

'Just dinner.'

'Will I meet you somewhere?'

'I'll pick you up. What's your address?'

Emily gave it to him while part of her mind was worrying about what to wear. Little black dress or colour? No. Not too much colour. Not red. Definitely not red. Red was too 'come and get me'. Pink was too girl-next-door. Did she have time to do her hair? Should she wash and blow-dry it or just scoop it up and hope for the best? Not too much make-up. Subtle and classy was best. Which heels? She needed heels because he was tall—a pair of stilts, even. A night of craning her neck to maintain eye contact would send her muscles into spasm.

'I would've called you before this but I was away on business.'

You still could have called me.

Was his 'business' a svelte blonde like the one she'd seen hanging off his arm when she'd searched him online? 'Really?'

'Yes. Really.'

Emily chewed at one side of her lower lip. Why *had* he called her? Hadn't she put him off with her 'marriage and kids' manifesto? Why had she blurted that out anyway? It was a first date no-no. Although, strictly speaking, it hadn't been a date at all. It had been a chance hook-up. An impulsive act she still couldn't explain. 'Why? I mean, it's not as if I'm your type.'

'Given your relationship with Allegra and mine with Draco, I wanted to make sure there wasn't any uncomfortableness about that night, in case we run into each other again because of our connection with them.'

There was going to be a whole heap of uncomfortableness when Emily told him what had resulted from that night. 'Right…good thinking.'

'I'll see you at seven.'

Emily didn't get a chance to say anything in reply for he ended the call. She stared at her phone, wondering if she should press redial, but then she realised he had a withheld number.

Her mother would say it was a sign.

* * *

Loukas clicked off his phone, placed it on his desk and leaned back in his office chair. He was breaking a rule by contacting Emily Seymour but he hadn't been able to get her out of his mind, or the memory of her touch out of his body.

One-night stands were meant to be exactly that. One night.

He had occasional relationships but he always kept things casual. Casual worked for him. Casual meant no emotional investment. Casual meant no promises he couldn't keep. He kept his relationships short, simple and based on sex.

But the sex didn't get much better than what he'd had with Emily. He wasn't sure what it was about her that had got him so worked up that night. She was cute in a girl-next-door way, with her petite frame and wavy shoulder-length hair that was neither blonde nor brown but a combination of the two. 'Bronde' she'd laughingly called it.

Her eyes were like a fawn's. Bambi eyes. Toffee-brown and dusted with dark spots that looked like tiny iron filings sprinkled over pools of honey. Her skin was peaches-and-cream and silk, with a scattering of freckles over the bridge of her retroussé nose that reminded him of a dusting of nutmeg. She had a sunny smile, bright and cheery with an endearing little overbite, and well-shaped lips built for kissing…and other things. Those other things had just about blown off the top of his head.

It was true she wasn't his type. But in another lifetime she might have been. In a parallel life where he didn't carry guilt like convict's chains. A life where every day he didn't relive the stomach-churning moment that had changed everything for his half-sister Ariana and had made him even more of an outcast in his family than he had been before. Even after seventeen years, every time he saw a child's bike his breath would stop and his guts would turn to gravy. If he heard the sudden squeal of brakes his heart would bang against his sternum like a wrecking ball. The siren of an ambulance sent his pulse sky-rocketing. He still lay awake at night hearing the crunch and crumple of metal and the piercing scream of a critically injured child…

Loukas knew he shouldn't be seeing Emily again. He shouldn't have hooked up with her in the first place. But, after having gone straight to the wedding from visiting Ariana in hospital after her latest bout of orthopaedic surgery, those chains of guilt had dug in with a cruel bite. He couldn't undo the past. It didn't matter how many times he relived that day. He had ruined his sister's life and destroyed his mother's second marriage in the process.

Emily's smile had been like a bolt of sunshine at the wedding. Her creamy cheeks had blushed when she'd first met his gaze. It had been a long time since he had been with a woman who blushed when he looked at her. He avoided that type usually. But something about Emily had drawn his interest, with her dancing eyes, neat little ballet dancer's figure and her cute clumsiness. Not to mention her adorable little bunny rabbit twitch where her nose would wrinkle up as if she had an invisible pair of glasses on and was trying to hitch them back up on the bridge of her nose.

He wasn't going to offer her anything but a temporary fling. He was only interested in the here and now. He was in London for a week working on some software for one of the government's security agencies. It was too good an opportunity to waste. A week-long fling to enjoy a little more of what they'd experienced that night. He would be upfront and honest about it. He wouldn't dress it up as anything other than what it was. He would offer her a no-strings, no-promises fling and leave it at that, just as he did with any other woman he took a fancy to.

And he had taken rather a fancy to Emily.

His mind kept going back to that night like a tongue going back to a niggling tooth. Loukas still wasn't sure why he'd taken her back to his room after Draco and Allegra's wedding. Emily had been staying on the same floor of Draco's private villa and he could easily have left her at her door after accompanying her back from the reception. But somehow the impersonal 'it was nice to meet you' kiss he'd intended to plant on her cheek had turned into something else. It was as if his lips had had their own agenda. They'd moved from her cheek to her lips like a missile finding a target.

Wham.

One kiss hadn't been enough. Her soft lips opening under his unleashed a ferocious desire from somewhere deep inside him. A desire that had swept away to some far-off, unreachable place every reason not to sleep with her.

They hadn't talked much—or at least, he hadn't. But then, that was his way. Talking had never been his currency in relationships. He was the strong, silent 'get on with the job' type. Emily, on the other hand, had talked of her fairy-tale dreams as though he'd been auditioning for the role of handsome prince.

As if that was ever going to happen.

But once it might have...

Loukas pushed out of his chair and turned to look out of the window to the motherboard-like grid of London's streets below. Crowds of people bustled about like busy ants. He was content with his life as it was…more or less. He had more money than he knew what to do with, a career that was global and a lifestyle that was enviable. It wasn't like him to leave it a month between lovers, but he hadn't been with anyone since Emily. He'd been over-the-top busy, certainly, but that didn't usually stop him from engaging in a bit of sex to relieve the tension with someone who was agreeable to his terms. Terms that didn't include anything long- or even mid-term. Short-term suited him because he could leave before things got too intense.

However, he didn't care for the term 'playboy' the press labelled him with because it suggested he was shallow and exploitative with women. In reality it was because he wanted to spare his partners unnecessary hurt. He wasn't like his father who moved from woman to woman with no regard for their feelings, promising them everything and then leaving them with nothing.

Loukas was the opposite. He promised them nothing and left them with generous gifts to soften the end of the affair.

But now the press's interest in him had gone up

a notch. With his best friend now off the market the focus had switched to him. Everywhere he went he had to be mindful of who was watching. The paparazzi were bad enough, but everyone had a camera phone these days, hankering after the money shot, so it was harder and harder to escape the intense interest in his private life.

Was it risky to see Emily again? Probably. But it was only for a week while he was in London. Seven days of sex without strings. The sex had been so damn good that night after the wedding. Good was an understatement. Everything about that night still reverberated in his body like a plucked cello string. He had only to think of her soft little hands with their butterfly touch to feel an aftershock roll through him. Just hearing her voice gave him goose bumps along the flesh of his spine. The soft breathlessness of it, the way she talked too much when she was nervous. The way she chewed at her lower lip and shielded her gaze with those spider-leg-long lashes. The way her cheeks pooled with pink as delicate as the blush of a rose.

He normally steered clear of sweet homespun girls like her. He always kept his head in relationships. Always. But just this once he wasn't listening to his head. His body was telling him to go for it.

And just this once that was exactly what he planned to do.

CHAPTER TWO

EMILY WAS JUST ABOUT to put her lip-gloss on when the doorbell rang. She grimaced at the state of her bathroom counter. Nearly every item of make-up or skincare treatment she owned was strewn about, some with the lids still open. Her bedroom was even worse. Clothes were on just about every surface, including the floor. It looked as if her room had been ransacked by an addict in frantic search of a fix.

She closed her bedroom door on the way past and opened the front door with a smile that fell a little short of the mark. 'Hi.'

Loukas's deep-brown gaze met hers in a look that sent a current of awareness through her body like a lightning strike on metal. 'Hello.'

How could a one-word greeting create such havoc with her senses? How could one man have such a potent effect on her? He was dressed in dark-blue trousers and a white shirt with a silver-and-black-striped tie and a navy-blue blazer, giving him an air of sophisticated man about town that was lethally attractive. Her pulse skipped and tripped at the mere sight of him. She opened the door wider, inching her feet back against the wall of the narrow hallway to give him more room. 'Would you like to come in for a bit? I'm not quite ready.' A hundred years wasn't enough time to get ready.

He stepped through the door without touching her but Emily felt as if he had. Her body tingled when he moved past her in the doorway, as if he had sent out a radar signal to every cell of her flesh. His tall frame shrank her hallway, the carriage-light fitting only just clearing the top of his head. The citrus notes of his aftershave swirled around her nostrils, the clean, sharp scent taking her back to that night in his arms. She had smelt him on her skin for hours afterwards. Felt his hard, male presence in her tender muscles for days. Every time she moved her body it reminded her of the glide and thrust of his body within hers.

The intimacy they'd shared that night was like a presence hovering. The air was charged with it. Electrified by it. Humming with it.

His bottomless brown gaze moved over her body like a caress. 'You look beautiful.'

Emily wished she didn't have such a propensity to blush. She could feel it crawling over her cheeks like a spill of red wine on a cream carpet. She tucked a strand of hair back behind her ear. Shifted her feet. Smoothed her hands down the front of her dress. 'Would you like a drink or...?'

He stepped closer, placing his hands on her waist and bringing his mouth down to within a breath of hers. 'Let's get this out of the way first.'

With a willpower Emily hadn't even known she possessed, she placed her hands against his chest and took a faltering step backwards. 'Can we have dinner first? It's just, it's been a month, and I feel a little...'

He gave one of his rare smiles. It was little more than an upward movement of his lips but it made something quiver on the floor of her belly like autumn leaves rustling in a playful breeze. 'You don't need to be nervous.'

Yes, I flipping well do.

Emily couldn't quite meet his gaze and focussed on the knot of his tie instead. 'Would you like to sit down? I just have to get my...my bag.'

And my courage, which seems to have left the building. Possibly the country.

'Take your time. The booking isn't till eight.'

'Right, well, then, I'll just be a moment.' She

backed away but bumped into the lamp on the table behind her. 'Oops. Sorry. Won't be a tick.'

Emily dashed back to the bathroom and gripped the edge of the basin.

You can do this. You can do this. You can do this.

She glanced at her reflection and stifled a groan. Was it her imagination or did she look a-vampire-just-left-me-for-dead pale? Maybe a bit more make-up would help. A bit of bronzer or something. She reached for her bronzer pad and brush but her hand knocked her bottle of perfume to the tiled floor with a glass-shattering crash. She looked at the shards of glass for a split second before she bent down to scoop them up, slicing one of her fingers in the process. Blood oozed down over her hand and wrist as if she was on the set of a horror movie. Footsteps sounded outside the bathroom, each one of them stepping on her flailing heart.

Boom. Boom. Boom.

'Are you okay in there?' Loukas asked, opening the door.

Emily grabbed the nearest hand towel and wrapped her hand in it. The smell of honeysuckle and vanilla was so strong and cloying it was nauseating. His nostrils quivered as if he thought so too. 'I—I broke my perfume bottle.'

He stepped closer and gently took her hand. 'Let me have a look. You might need stitches.'

She watched with one eye squinted while he carefully unpeeled her makeshift bandage. He held her hand to the light, his eyes narrowed in focus, his strong eyebrows drawn together in concentration. 'No stitches needed, but I think there's a sliver of glass in there. Do you have some tweezers?'

What a question to ask a girl with eyebrows that grew faster than weeds. 'In the cupboard above the basin.'

He opened the cupboard and took the tweezers from the bottom shelf next to her jumbo pack of tampons.

Won't need those for a while.

He rinsed the tweezers under the hot tap and then ran some antiseptic he'd found on the middle shelf over them.

Emily braced herself for the sting but his touch was so gentle she barely noticed anything except the way he was standing close enough for her to feel his body warmth. Close enough to smell the sharp notes of citrus in his aftershave, redolent of sun-warmed lemons and limes. Close enough to see the pinpricks of dark stubble peppered over his lean jaw, hinting at the potent male hormones surging in his blood.

Stop thinking about his surging blood.
I can't help it!

He glanced at her. 'I'm not hurting you too much?'

'No...' Emily looked at his mouth, the way it curved around his words, the way the stubble surrounded it, making her fingers ache to reach up and trace it.

He went back to work on her finger, gently removing the shard of glass and cleansing the wound with another wash of antiseptic. He reached back to the cupboard for a plaster and a small crepe bandage, which he placed on her finger. 'There you go,' he said with another heart-stopping, upward movement of his lips. 'Good as new.'

Emily was so dazed by his almost-smile and his closeness she didn't register what he was doing for a moment. It was only when he stepped past her to place the plaster and bandage wrappings in the metal pedal bin next to her that her heart came to a screeching standstill. She quickly blocked him from accessing the bin, as if she were guarding the Hope Diamond. 'D-don't put it in there.' She held out her good hand, not one bit surprised it was shaking. 'I'll take it and put it in the bin in the kitchen.'

One of his eyebrows rose like a question mark. 'Why not this bin?'

She forced herself to hold his gaze, her heart beating so hard it was as if there were panicked pigeons and a handful of hummingbirds trapped in her chest. 'This one's…erm…full.'

His eyes moved back and forth between each of hers. 'What's wrong? You seem a little jumpy.'

'I'm not jumpy.'

Probably shouldn't have answered so quickly.

He reached out his hand and trailed the backs of his bent knuckles down the slope of her cheek, making every nerve fizz and whizz. His eyes went to her mouth, lingering there as if he was reliving every time he had kissed her that night a month ago. 'Why do I make you so nervous?'

Emily swallowed loud enough to hear it. 'I'm n-not nervous…'

Loukas inched up her chin, the pad of his thumb moving in slow mesmerising circles, his eyes holding hers. 'I couldn't stop thinking about that night. How good it was between us.'

She sent her tongue out to moisten her lips that were as dry as the crepe bandage on her finger. 'Isn't it always good between you and your lovers?'

He gave a shrug but there was no hint of arrogance about it. 'Mostly. What about you?'

Emily tried but failed to suppress a snort. 'I can count my previous lovers on half a hand. My mother's had more sex than me. She's *still* having more than me.'

He continued to look at her without speaking, his eyes holding hers as if he found her fascinating. But then, maybe a twenty-nine-year-old almost-virgin was something of an enigma to him.

'She's a relationships therapist,' Emily said into the silence. 'She teaches people how to have better relationships by working on their sex lives. Ironic that her daughter's sex life is practically non-existent.'

Here you go again. Telling him all your stuff.

So? I need to break the ice a bit. I can't just tell him he's going to be a dad without a bit of a lead up.

You are so unsophisticated!

His hands came to settle on her waist, his eyes sexily hooded. 'Maybe I can help you with that.'

The warmth of his hands seemed to be travelling right through her clothes, through every layer of her skin, sending electric pulses down her nerves until they were twitching in excitement. Her inner core registered his proximity like a scanner recognises a code. It was as though she were micro-chipped for him and him alone. Her intimate muscles were clenching, contracting, wanting.

'I haven't had a lot of luck with men,' Emily said.

'I had one lover before my ex, but it hardly counts, as it was over before I blinked. I was with Daniel seven years so it's left me a little out of the game, so to speak.'

Argh! What are you doing? You're making yourself sound like some sort of relationship tragic.

But I don't want him to think I've been jumping every man I meet.

His hands went from her waist to skim up her arms and rest on her shoulders. His eyes had a lustrous depth to them that reminded her of a bottomless lake. 'You haven't had a lover since Daniel? Apart from me, I mean?'

'No. I dated a few times but it never came to anything. I suspect that was why I was so…so enthusiastic when you kissed me outside my room,' Emily said. 'I hope I didn't shock you.'

Loukas brushed his thumb over her lower lip. 'You delighted and surprised me.'

That's me. Full of delightful surprises.

She stretched her lips into a rictus smile. 'Erm… there's something we need to discuss…'

'I'm not in this for the long haul, Emily.' His mouth had an intractable set to it. 'I want you to be clear on that right from the outset. I'm only here in London this week, so if we have a fling that's all it will be. A fling. Nothing else.'

'I understand that. It's just there's some—'

'I want you.' His voice hummed in her core as deep as a bass chord.

Emily placed her hands flat against his chest, her hips bumping into his, sending a shockwave of tingly awareness through her body. She couldn't think when he was this close. Her body went on autopilot. Wanting. Craving. Hungering. Her breasts tingled with the memory of his touch, the heat and fire of his lips and tongue and the sexy scrape of his teeth. He was so magnetic. So irresistible. So tempting her inner core was contracting with little pulses of lust, as if recalling the sexy thrust of his body within hers.

How could she possibly be thinking about sex at a time like this? But it seemed her body could only think about sex when Loukas was within touching distance. His chest was hard and warm under her hands, the clean, laundered scent of his shirt filling her nostrils. The length and strength of his thighs so close to her own reminded her of how those muscle-packed legs had entrapped hers in a tangle of sheets, taking her to a sensual heaven she hadn't known existed. Her body remembered everything about that encounter. Remembered and begged for it to be repeated. The drumming of her pulse echoed in her core, making her aware of every inch of her body where it was in contact with his, as though all the nerves on those spots had been supercharged.

His mouth came down to hover above hers, his warm, minty breath sending her senses reeling. 'Tell me you want me.'

'I want you, but there's…' Emily stepped back from him, using what little willpower she had left, but she stumbled over the pedal bin behind her left foot and it tipped over and spilled its contents in front of his Italian-leather-clad feet.

An unpinned grenade would have had a similar effect.

Loukas's face drained of colour as if he were the one with morning sickness. He stood frozen for a moment. Totally statue-like—as if someone had pressed a pause button on him. Then he swallowed.

Once.

Twice.

Three times.

Each one of them was clearly audible in the pregnant silence—*no pun intended*. Emily watched as if in slow motion when he bent to pick up not one, but seven test wands. He examined the tell-tale blue lines, the wands clanking against each other like chopsticks.

His eyes finally cut to hers, sharp, flint-hard with query. 'You're…*pregnant?*'

He said the word as though it was the most shocking diagnosis anyone could have. Up until a few hours ago, she had thought so too.

Emily wrung her hands like a distraught heroine from a period drama, wincing when her damaged finger protested. 'I was trying to tell you but—'

'Is it mine?' The question was a verbal slap.

She double blinked. 'Of course it's yours. I—'

'But we used condoms.' The suspicion in his voice scraped at her already overwrought nerves.

'I know, but condoms sometimes fail, and this time one must have—'

'Aren't you on the pill?' His brows were so tightly drawn above his eyes it gave him an intimidating air.

'I—I was taking a break from it.' Emily could feel tears welling up. The concentrated smell of her spilt perfume was making her feel queasy. Her fingertips were fizzing as if her blood were being filtered through coarse sand. The tingling sensation spread to her arms, travelling all the way up to her neck, making it hard to keep her head steady. The room began to spin, the floor to shift beneath her feet as though she were standing on a pitching boat deck. She reached blindly for the edge of the bathroom counter but it was like a ghost hand reaching through fog. Every one of her limbs folded as if she were a marionette with severed strings. She heard Loukas call out her name through a vacuum and then everything faded to black…

'Emily!' Loukas dropped to his knees in front of her slumped form, his heart banging against his chest wall like a bell struck by a madman. Her face was as white as the basin above her collapsed form, her skin clammy. He brushed the sticky hair back from her forehead, his mind still whirling with the news of her pregnancy.

Pregnant.

The word struck another hammer-like blow to his chest. A baby. *His* baby. How had it happened? He was always so careful. Paranoid careful. He never had sex without a condom. He never took risks. Never. How could he have got her pregnant? It had been a bit low of him to suggest it wasn't his, but panic had blunted his sensitivity.

A father?

Him?

Why hadn't he asked her about contraception? If he'd known she wasn't on the pill, or using a hormone implant device, he would have taken extra caution. He couldn't be a father. He didn't want to be a father. He had never planned to be a father. Panic drummed through him like wildebeests in stampede. He tried to picture himself with a baby and his mind went blank, his chest seizing with dread, vice-like. His intestines knotted as though they were being sectioned by twine.

No. Not him. Not now. Not ever.

He looked at Emily's slumped form and another dagger of guilt jabbed him. Hard. He had done this, upsetting her to the point of collapse. She had been trying to tell him something but he'd been so intent on squaring up their fling he hadn't given her a chance. No wonder she had acted so nervous and on edge.

She was pregnant.

With *his* baby.

What was he going to do? What was the *right* thing to do? Hands-off provision for his child seemed a little tacky somehow. There was no way he could walk away from this. He would have to be involved with his child as he wished his father had been for him. He would have to be responsible for the child. To provide for and protect it. The thought of protecting a child was enough to make Loukas break out in another prickly sweat.

How could *he* keep a child safe?

He had got Emily pregnant. Some would call it an accident, a freakish trick of fate, or destiny or whatever, but he blamed himself. He had slipped up. He had done what he had sworn he would never do.

He was to become a father, unless she chose to get rid of it.

He allowed the thought some traction, but as escape hatches went it wasn't one he felt comfortable with. It would be Emily's decision, certainly, but he hoped she wouldn't feel pressured into it because of their circumstances. He would have to make it clear he was okay with her keeping it. More than okay, even if he harboured more doubts than a sceptics' conference. Not doubts about keeping the baby—doubts about himself as a father.

His own father had insisted a recent partner have an abortion after she'd fallen pregnant, and when she'd refused he'd summarily dumped her. The young woman had subsequently attempted suicide and lost the baby as a result. She had recently been paid a large sum of money by a gossip magazine for a tell-all interview about how Loukas's father had caused her so much distress. The interview, by association, had put the spotlight on Loukas and the way he conducted his relationships, especially now he was attracting more media attention than ever before.

But there was no way he would ever put that sort of pressure on any woman. Emily's pregnancy was a shock, a surprise and an inconvenience, but there was a tiny human life in the making, and he would not do or say anything to compromise that development, nor the mental health of its mother.

He was angry with himself for putting Emily in this situation. Furious. Ashamed. Deeply, thoroughly ashamed that he had acted on impulse and slept with her when normally he would have steered clear of an unworldly woman like her. He'd been the one to make the first move. He hadn't been able to keep his eyes off her, much less his hands. He had foolishly thought he could have a one-night stand and walk away. He should have walked away from her at her bedroom door at Draco's villa—that was what he should have done.

What had he been thinking, sleeping with a cute little homespun girl like her? She wasn't his type and he certainly wasn't hers. He wasn't a rake, but he was no altar boy either. It had been a night of out-of-character madness and now it had come to this. A life had been created that would link them together for ever.

How could he walk away from this? This was his doing and he would have to face it even though it was like facing his worst nightmare. Panic wrapped steel cords around his chest, squeezing the very breath out of him. Sweat broke out over his brow.

The roots of his hair prickled as if ants were playing hide and seek on his scalp.

Why couldn't he press replay on his life and do everything differently? How many times had he wished that? Every time he saw his sister's damaged body he wished he could turn back time. Now he had another regret to hang on his conscience. But, unlike with his sister and mother, whom he kept at a respectful distance, given the dreadful impact he'd had on their lives, he could not so easily distance himself from his own child.

A child who would grow up and call him Daddy. A child who would look up to him. A child who would expect certain things of him—things he wasn't capable of giving. How could he be trusted with a child's welfare when he had already ruined one innocent child's life?

Emily groaned and slowly opened her eyes. She looked at him blankly for a moment and then she captured her lower lip with her teeth and lowered her gaze. 'I'm sorry...'

'No.' His voice caught on the word and he had to clear his throat to continue. 'I'm the one who's sorry. Are you okay? Shall I get you a glass of water?'

She made to get up and Loukas helped her into a sitting position to allow time for her blood pressure to go back to normal. 'I'm fine. I just need a minute.'

'Should I call a doctor?' He began to reach for his phone but she put a hand on his arm.

'No, I'm fine, really.' Her hand melted away from his arm and went back to her lap. The sound of her fingertips flicking against each other made him realise how nervous she was.

'Have you seen a doctor at all?'

She shook her head. 'Not yet. I wanted to do a few tests first.'

Loukas glanced at the seven test wands, wondering how many more she'd planned to take.

When he looked back at her she gave him a self-deprecating grimace. 'I know,' she said. 'Overkill.' After a moment she added, 'We can do a paternity test if you'd—'

'No,' Loukas said, surprising himself with the strength of his conviction. 'That won't be necessary.'

Her eyes shimmered and her throat rose and fell over a swallow. 'Thank you for believing me. It means…a lot…'

He brushed his hand over her hair and then tucked a couple of strands back behind her ear as if she were six years old. She gave him a tremulous movement of her lips that loosely could have been described as a smile. 'You can't be very far along,' he said. 'Isn't it too early to be sure one way or the other?'

'The tests are pretty accurate these days. They can pick up the slightest change in hormonal activity within a few days of conception.'

'What do you plan to do?' As soon as he asked it he wished he hadn't phrased it quite that way. It sounded as if he considered the baby to be a problem to be removed. Eradicated. Deleted like an incorrect digit in a code.

Her eyes took on a determined spark, her normally plump mouth now a tight line. 'I'm keeping it, so please don't try and convince me otherwise, because I don't need your help. I'm perfectly able to do this on my own. I just thought you should know, that's all.'

'I'm sorry. I wasn't suggesting you should get rid of it,' Loukas said.

She angled him a look that reminded him of a detective nailing a suspect. 'Weren't you?'

He released a jagged breath. 'I can't deny I'm a little shocked by the news. More than shocked. If I'm not acting with the sensitivity and enthusiasm of a normal father-to-be, then you'll have to forgive me. I never planned to be a father.'

Emily clambered to her feet, brushing off his offer of assistance. 'Then why haven't you had a vasectomy? Then you could rule a line under the subject permanently.'

He'd thought of it. Several times. He hadn't avoided it out of cowardice, or squeamishness, or out-dated notions on masculinity. He didn't know what it was but something had made him shy away from the decision to render himself infertile. 'I haven't got around to it yet.'

'Maybe you should before someone else ends up pregnant.'

Loukas was ashamed he hadn't yet thought of what this was like for her. Sure, she'd said she wanted marriage and kids, but he'd got the impression she wanted them in that order. Marriage first. Kids later. Having a child was a huge responsibility for a woman under any circumstances—a life-changing responsibility. 'Emily...are you okay with this? With being pregnant?'

Her eyes fell away from his as if she couldn't bear to look at him. 'I wasn't at first. I was in denial until I did the seventh test. I didn't want to be like my mother. Pregnant outside of marriage to a guy she had a one-night stand with. It was like a nightmare.'

'And now?'

Her good hand crept to her abdomen, resting on it as though she were protecting a baby bird.

'It's not the baby's fault it wasn't planned. I'll cope. Somehow.'

'I'll support you in any way I can. You know that, surely? You and the baby will want for nothing.'

'I'm not after your money, Loukas.' Her eyes came back to his. 'I just wanted our baby to know its father. I've never met mine. I don't even know who he is and he has no idea I even exist. Even my mother isn't sure who he is.'

Loukas could hear the regret in her voice. He wasn't close to his own father but at least he knew who he was and he shared his surname. Which brought him up against another huge stumbling block. Marriage. The only way his child could legally have his name would be for him to marry Emily. He wasn't against marriage per se. It was an institution he believed in—for other people. People unlike him who didn't have the sort of baggage he was lugging around. Baggage that still gave him sweat-slicked nightmares. Baggage he couldn't get rid of because his half-sister Ariana lived with the consequences of what he'd done every single day of her life.

A sharp-clawed fist clutched at his gut.

Marriage?

To a girl he had only met a month ago? A girl

who was now carrying his child? A girl he hadn't been able to get out of his mind because she was sweet, clumsy and shy.

Could he do it? Could he sacrifice his freedom for the sake of a child he had never planned to have?

He had a responsibility towards his child. He wasn't the sort of man to shirk responsibility. That was what his father was like, but not him. He faced up to problems. Assessed them. Dealt with them. Conquered them.

He could provide money without marriage, plenty of money, although having contact with the child would be tricky if he wasn't living under the same roof. He wanted to be involved but had no idea how to go about it without marrying Emily. He had seen too many fathers, including his own, who provided everything money could buy but gave nothing of themselves. He didn't want to be that sort of father, but he didn't know how to conduct a relationship—any relationship—except at arm's length.

'We should marry as soon as possible.'

'Don't be ridiculous,' Emily said. 'No one has to get married because of pregnancy these days. Even couples in love don't always get married when they have a child together.'

'I want to be a part of my child's life,' Loukas said. 'I want him or her to have my name.'

'They can still have your name. But I'd only like you to be involved if that's what you want. A child can tell if its parent wants to be around them or not.'

Loukas wondered about the dynamic between Emily and her mother. There seemed a subtext to her words that hinted at some tension. 'I'll do whatever I can to support you, Emily. You can trust me on that.'

Her gaze met his. 'Will you publically acknowledge the baby as yours when it's born? Or would you prefer me to keep it a secret to protect your privacy?'

Loukas frowned. There was no way he was going to disown his own flesh and blood. Not like his father, who had insisted on a paternity test and then, when it had come out positive, still insisted the poor woman get rid of his baby. 'Of course I'll acknowledge it. This is my mistake, not the child's. I accept full responsibility for it.'

'Then please don't insult me by asking me to marry you,' she said with a look hard enough to crack a nut.

Loukas wondered what had happened to the girl who couldn't wait to get married and have babies.

Four kids and an Irish Retriever, if his memory served him correctly. Why then wasn't she grasping at this chance to land herself a rich husband? Though he hadn't taken her for a gold-digger. That was what had most appealed to him about her the day of the wedding. She had a guileless innocence about her. She reminded him of a friendly puppy who wanted to be loved by everyone.

But what was insulting about his proposal of marriage? He could think of hundreds, possibly thousands, of women who would jump at the chance of a proposal from him. The more he thought about it, the more he felt that marriage was the best option all round. It would give him the best chance of supporting her and the baby. It wasn't as if it would have any of the toxic elements of his parents' marriage. Emily and he were not in love with each other, so the marriage could be drawn up as a parenting contract. A formalised parenting contract that gave them the benefits of marriage without the emotional baggage of a normal relationship.

He would broach the topic again once she was feeling a little better, but this time he would lay out what was going to happen: a convenient mid-term marriage to parent their child. Perfect solution. 'Do you need anything now? Some money to buy baby stuff or—'

'No, I haven't needed to buy anything yet...' The colour drained out of her face again and she wobbled on her feet as if the floor was uneven. She put a hand to her forehead. 'I—I think I might have to give dinner a miss. I'm going to lie down for a bit...'

Loukas lunged forward and caught her before she hit the floor. Emily folded like a rag doll in his arms, her chalk-white face lolling to rest against the wall of his chest. 'Are you okay?'

'Feeling a bit faint...'

He reached for his phone with his free hand, the other keeping her close. 'I'm going to call an ambulance.'

She pushed back against him, her eyes troubled. 'No, please don't do that. I'll be fine in a minute or two.'

What about in half an hour? Later that night? The following morning? Who was going to take care of her, to watch over her, to make sure she didn't faint and hurt herself? He couldn't leave her like this. What if she had a fall? She could end up with a brain injury or worse. She was his responsibility now. The knowledge cemented his decision to marry her. How else could he keep a close eye on her if he lived in another country, or even a few streets away? No. This was the only way forward. 'Do you want to lie down? Here, I'll carry you.'

He scooped her up and carried her to her bedroom. It looked like someone had ransacked the
room or got dressed for a night out in the middle
of a hurricane. The wardrobe was open and a va-
riety of clothes strewn about, some on the end of
the bed, others draped over a chair and more on the
floor. The dressing table was scattered with make-
up detritus: brushes, pots, hair products and a hair
straightener. He laid her slight figure on the bed.

She lay back, folded her bandaged hand over her
forehead and closed her eyes. 'I'm so sorry about
this.'

Loukas took her good hand and stroked her slen-
der nail-bitten fingers. 'Don't be silly. It's not your
fault.'

It's mine.

CHAPTER THREE

IN THE END Loukas decided against calling an ambulance. But, as soon as Emily's dizziness passed, he insisted on taking her to hospital. Hospitals were not his favourite places, with their palpable sense of urgency. The lights, the sounds, the smells, and the nerve-jangling scream of sirens as the ambulances came rocketing into the receiving bay, made his heart threaten to beat its way out of his ribcage. It brought back the memory of the afternoon when his sister had been rushed to hospital, clinging to life.

But he wanted Emily checked out.

She, however, was not so keen on the idea.

She stood with her arms folded and her heels dug into the carpet beside her bed as if someone had glued her to the floor. 'But I don't need to go to hospital.'

'You fainted twice in the space of half an hour,' Loukas said. 'I'm not leaving you on your own until

I get you checked out. What if you fainted in the middle of the night and hit your head and got a brain injury?'

She pouted like a small, obstinate child. 'You're being ridiculous. First suggesting marriage and now a trip to the emergency department. The staff will think I'm crazy. Pregnancy isn't a disease, you know.'

'I want that finger checked out,' he said, trying another tack. 'It needs to be looked at under ultrasound in case there are any fragments in there. If you got blood poisoning it would be disastrous for the baby.'

Her face suddenly fell. 'Oh…'

He held out his hand and she silently slipped hers into it. He closed his fingers around her hand, privately marvelling at how small it was compared to his. But everything about her was tiny. He felt like a giant next to her. She barely made it up to his shoulder in heels and he could just about span her waist with his hands. Not that he would be able to do it once her pregnancy started to show. He still couldn't get his head around the fact she was pregnant. Inside her womb his DNA was getting it on with hers and making a baby.

His baby.

The thought of bringing a child into the world

that he would be totally responsible for made his head pound with dread. What if he screwed up? It wasn't easy being a parent even when you planned to be one. He had no idea how to be a father. He was hopeless at familial relationships. He kept people at a distance. Even the people who mattered to him he kept at arm's length.

That was why casual relationships worked so well for him. There were no emotional expectations. No closeness. No bonding. No one got hurt. What if he hurt his child? Not physically, but emotionally? Didn't kids need close emotional bonds with their parents to thrive and reach their full potential? He had been close to his mother until his father got sole custody of him in a bitter divorce, only to dump him in an English boarding school when he got tired of being a single parent. After years of living so far away from his mother, Loukas hadn't been able to rebuild the relationship to the way it had been before. He knew it hadn't been his mother's fault. She had done everything in her power to make him feel loved and wanted.

It was he who was the problem.

He'd never wanted to be that vulnerable again. To need someone so much, only to have them ripped away from you. He had taught himself not to need. These days the only needs he had were physical, and he dealt with them efficiently and somewhat perfunctorily, which was probably why the sex with Emily had stood out in a long list of impersonal hook-ups. Stood out so much he could still feel it in his body, the erotic echo of it moving through his flesh like aftershocks if he so much as touched her.

But, while marrying her would solve one problem, he was too well aware it could stir up others. He would offer commitment but not love. The concept of loving someone made all those childhood demons come back to haunt and taunt him: *you love them, you lose them. You love them, you hurt them.* He would be committed for as long as their marriage lasted but he would not—*could not*—promise anything else.

Loukas tucked Emily into his car and made sure she was comfortable before he took his place behind the steering wheel. 'I haven't finished with the topic of marriage,' he said, glancing at her as he turned over the engine. 'It's the best option going forward.'

She flicked him an irritated glance. 'You know what? I'm going to ignore that. I did not hear you say the M word.'

Loukas had never felt more serious about something. It was the perfect solution and he wasn't going to back away from it. 'We'll make a formal announcement after we get you checked out.'

'You can't force people to marry you, Loukas. You just can't do that.'

Don't be so sure about that.

Emily was embarrassed about turning up at Accident and Emergency when there was essentially nothing wrong with her. The waiting room was full of sick and injured people much worse off than her, but Loukas had insisted, and had all but bundled her into his top-of-the-range hire car, casting her worried glances all the way to hospital as if she was going to expire right there in front of him. Not only had he insisted on taking her to hospital, but he'd also returned to the subject of marriage with a steely determination that was a little terrifying, to say the least. Surely he wasn't serious? She hadn't had the energy to argue with him back in the car. The nausea and dizziness had made it impossible for her to string two lucid thoughts together, and the thought of marrying Loukas Kyprianos was a thought a long way from being lucid.

But, when they walked into the reception area, it looked as if Loukas was the one who was ill. He went a ghastly grey colour and his hand where it was holding hers became slick with sweat. 'Are you all right?' Emily asked, glancing up at him.

'I'm fine.' He spoke the words through lips that barely moved, as if he was trying to conserve energy.

'You look awfully pale.'

He slanted her a wry look. 'You should talk.'

'Can I help you?' asked the weary-looking receptionist.

'My…er…fiancée needs to see a doctor,' Loukas said.

Fiancée?

Emily rounded her gaze on him and mouthed, *'What the hell?'*

The receptionist glanced at Emily's bandaged finger. 'For your finger?'

'That and…something else,' Loukas said, pulling at his shirt collar as if it was too tight.

Emily moved closer to the reception window. 'I didn't want to come in but Loukas insisted.'

'What seems to be the problem?' the receptionist asked.

'I'm…pregnant.'

'Are you bleeding?'

'No.'

The receptionist handed Emily a form on a clipboard and a pen dangling on a string. 'Fill out the patient details and someone will be with you shortly.'

Emily sat beside Loukas and painstakingly filled in the form, but she was conscious of him sitting there in a state of barely disguised agitation. He shifted his feet, crossed and uncrossed his ankles. Pushed them back underneath the chair, only to bring them out again. He rubbed at the back of his neck. He loosened his tie. Then he sat forward with his elbows on his knees and his head in his hands.

And so he should sweat. What was he thinking, pulling that *'my fiancée'* stunt on her? Did he think she'd be too embarrassed to correct him?

Then why didn't you correct him?

I was too embarrassed.

You could correct him now.

In front of all these people in the waiting room?

Better do it sooner rather than later.

Emily anchored the pen under the clip on the clipboard with a resounding click and placed it on the vacant seat on her left. 'Can you sit still, or is that your conscience niggling at you?'

He swivelled his head to look at her. 'I hate hospitals.'

'Well, maybe if you hadn't told the receptionist we're engaged, you wouldn't be feeling so rotten.' She kept her voice at a stage whisper because she was conscious of the other patients sitting nearby. 'But I suppose you only did that because you knew I'd be too embarrassed to make a scene. But once we get out of here I'm going to give you a piece of my mind.'

He glanced at the clock on the wall and gave an exaggerated eye roll. '*If* we ever get out of here.'

Emily winced at the time that had already elapsed. Where had the last hour and a half gone? 'I hope it won't be too long. You can go if you like. I can catch a cab after I'm—'

'No. I'm staying with you and that's the end of it.' He jerked his sleeve up to glance at his watch, presumably to check if the one on the wall was lying, and then sat back against the plastic chair with a thump. 'How long is "shortly", for God's sake?'

'I once waited six and a half hours for a splinter in my foot to be removed when I was ten,' Emily said. 'My mum left me for most of it to go to an astrology workshop. I got the nurse to call her when I was done.'

Loukas turned to look at her, his brows drawn together in a tight frown. 'Are you close to her?'

Emily shrugged and shifted her gaze to stare at the linoleum on the floor. 'Aren't all girls close to their mums?'

'Have you told her about the—'

'Not yet. But she's not the maternal type, so the prospect of being a granny won't have her rushing off for a pair of knitting needles any time soon.'

Emily suddenly noticed that the two women sitting opposite them in the waiting room were glancing in their direction. The woman on the left nudged her friend and pointed at Loukas. Emily wasn't game enough to look at Loukas but she sensed him stiffening in the chair beside her. She sank a little lower in her chair, wishing she could disappear before the women asked for verification. How much had they heard of her conversation with Loukas? She'd kept her voice low, but what if they'd overheard her talking about their 'engagement' or the baby? She wasn't used to being examined. Was this what Loukas had to live with? The constant scrutiny of his private life would be torture for someone as reserved as him.

The woman's companion pulled up something on her phone screen and seemed to compare it to Loukas. 'It's Loukas Kyprianos all right,' she said, loud enough for half the waiting room to hear. 'The Greek billionaire friend of Draco Papandreou. Did you hear the girl with him say she's pregnant? Quick—take a photo.'

The click of the camera phone was as loud as a rifle shot.

Loukas didn't move. Emily cast him a covert glance but his features were schooled into an impassive mask, except for a tiny muscle in his jaw that was twitching as if it was being randomly zapped by an invisible electrode.

The woman who had taken the photo spoke again. 'Let's hope he doesn't do what his jerk of a father did when he got his young girlfriend pregnant.'

'Yeah, I read about that. Awful business, wasn't it? But the girl got paid a fortune for that interview. Good on her, I say. Who wouldn't want to be compensated after what that lowlife put her through?'

What awful business?

Emily's ears weren't just out on stalks but on scaffolding and in a high-wire harness too. What had Loukas's father done to his pregnant girlfriend? He sounded like an absolute cad. Was that why Loukas was making such a big deal about marrying, so no one would think he was anything like his disreputable father?

The nurse called Emily's name at that point and Loukas stood and guided Emily out of the waiting room with brisk efficiency. 'What happened with your—' she began.

'Later.' The word was clipped out through white, tight lips and he led her into the cubicle to wait for the doctor.

The curtain twitched aside and a doctor came,

who did a double-take when she saw Loukas. 'Oh, my God, Loukas? Fancy seeing you here.'

Was there anyone in the whole of London who *didn't* know who Loukas was? Emily glanced at him to see if he was as excited as the young doctor but his face was blank. 'I'm sorry, do I know you?' he said.

The doctor's smile faded a little. 'We had a drink together at a charity function last year here in London. Don't you remember? Maida Freeman's my name. We were going to catch up later but I got called away to an emergency. I was on call.' She rolled her eyes. 'Story of my life.'

'Of course I remember,' Loukas said with a polite movement of his lips that didn't involve his eyes or his teeth.

Dr Freeman turned to Emily. 'Such a small world.'

Not small enough if I'm going to run into a host of his ex- or would-be lovers.

'What can I do for you?'

'I didn't want to bother anyone but Loukas insisted on—' Emily began.

'Emily fainted this evening. Twice,' Loukas said. 'She's…pregnant.' He swallowed audibly between the two words.

'That's quite common in early pregnancy,' Dr

Freeman said. 'Dizziness, light-headedness, faint-ing, nausea and vomiting, as the hormones do their thing. I'll get the nurse to do some obs and we'll take some blood to make sure you're not anaemic.' Her gaze honed in on Emily's bandaged finger. 'What happened to your finger?'

'I cut it on some broken glass.'

The doctor's gaze seemed to sharpen. 'How are you feeling about the pregnancy?'

'What do you mean?' Emily asked.

'Was it planned or…?'

'Not planned but very much welcomed,' Loukas said, reaching for Emily's good hand and holding it within the warm cage of his.

Welcomed?

Emily did her best to disguise her shock.

But then the doctor looked between Loukas and her and, finally settling her gaze on Loukas, smiled again. 'I'm really happy for you, Loukas. I'm sure you'll make an excellent father.'

Unlike your own.

The doctor didn't say it out loud, probably be-cause she was too much of a professional, but the words seemed to hover there in the silence all the same. Emily felt as though she were on stage in a play on opening night, but having been given the wrong script. She didn't know anything about

Loukas other than he was Draco Papandreou's best friend. She didn't know what his favourite colour was. She didn't know what books he liked to read or what movies he watched. She didn't know what political persuasion he had or anything about his childhood other than his parents had divorced when he was a kid. And she had learned that from Allegra.

'How long have you been a couple?' Dr Freeman asked.

There was another beat of silence. 'We've been keeping it a secret for a while,' Loukas said before she could answer. 'I met Emily through my best friend from university.'

The doctor smiled again. 'Ah yes, he got married recently, didn't he? I read about it in the press. I guess you two will be getting hitched too, now you're going to be parents?'

'We don't—' Emily began.

'Yes,' Loukas said, squeezing Emily's hand. 'The plans are already afoot.'

'Oh, that's lovely,' the doctor said. 'I'm a bit old-fashioned in that way. I reckon kids need to know their parents are committed enough to marry each other. It gives them a sense of security, in my opinion. Now, let me have a look at that finger of yours.'

The doctor examined the wound and ordered an

ultrasound to make sure there was no further debris. The machine came in on a portable trolley with a radiology attendant. 'Just the hand at this stage,' the doctor said. 'It's a little early to see the baby unless we do a vaginal ultrasound. If we weren't so busy tonight I'd order one for you.'

'No, that's okay,' Emily said. 'I'll wait until later.'

The hand was given the all-clear and the radiology staffer wheeled the trolley out. A nurse came in and took blood while the doctor saw to another patient in the next cubicle. There wasn't enough privacy to talk to Loukas but Emily sent him a speaking look. If he thought he could railroad her into marriage, then he was in for a big surprise.

The doctor came back a short time later with a bottle of iron supplements and an information sheet for maternal health and maternity services. 'You're all good to go. Have plenty of rest and try to eat small meals when you can. If the nausea and vomiting increase or become chronic, then see your GP as soon as you can.' She smiled again at Loukas. 'You did the right thing, bringing her in. It shows how much you care about her. Believe me, I see all types in here, and the behaviour of some fathers-to-be towards their partner would make your hair fall out.'

'Thanks for taking care of her,' Loukas said. 'I appreciate it.'

* * *

Emily walked out of the hospital with Loukas beside her. 'I can't believe you told her we're getting married,' she said once they were clear of the busy entrance and on their way to his car. 'Not only Dr Freeman, but the receptionist as well. Are you nuts? What if they tell someone?'

'They're meant to keep patient information confidential,' he said.

She stopped walking to look up at him. 'And what about everyone else in that emergency department? What about those women in the waiting room? They recognised you. They took a photo of you. They've probably sold it to one of those media sites by now.'

His features gave a tight spasm. 'If it happens, it happens.'

'But why say we're engaged when we're—'

'We're what?' he said. 'Virtual strangers? How do you think that would've made you look?'

Emily blinked. 'Oh...'

'Exactly.' He let out a short breath. 'You've come out of a long-term relationship only to get pregnant after a one-night stand. It's not fair, but women still get frowned on for stuff like that. I figured it was best to let Dr Freeman think we've known each other for a while and were planning to marry.'

Emily could see his point and was unexpectedly touched he'd considered the impact on her reputation. But she suspected his motives were not entirely about protecting her reputation. Loukas wanted to marry her and was refusing to take no for an answer. She hadn't taken him for a my-way-or-the-highway guy, but then she was hardly an expert when it came to reading men. She had been with Daniel for seven years and had never once suspected he was interested in men instead.

Once they were inside Loukas's car and on their way, she swivelled in her seat to look at him. 'So, what was the business with your father those women in the waiting room spoke of?'

His mouth tightened as if invisible stitches were being tugged from inside his jaw. 'Nothing.'

'It can't have been nothing if those strangers know about it,' Emily said. 'And Dr Freeman didn't say anything but I could read the subtext. Don't you think I should know too, since I'm now apparently—' she made air quotes with her fingers '—engaged to you?'

He blew out another breath, longer this time, and his hands gripped the steering wheel firmly, as if he was worried it was going to be snatched away from him. 'He got a partner pregnant earlier this year. She was nineteen years old. He insisted she have an abortion and when she refused he dumped her.' His knuckles and tendons showed white through the tan of his skin. 'She tried to kill herself by slashing her wrists soon after. Someone found her in time but not in time to save the baby. There was too much blood loss. She miscarried on the way to hospital.'

'Oh, that's terrible…'

'My father is a high-profile businessman here and in the US, and of course the press love salacious stories like that,' he said. 'The young woman got offered a large sum of money for a tell-all interview. I can't say I blame her, but it's made my life difficult, because everyone's waiting to pounce on a "like father, like son" follow-up story.'

Emily could see the invidious position Loukas was in with her pregnancy. No wonder he'd insisted on marriage. He would be keen to avoid any remote comparison with his father. But marriage was meant to be a sacred commitment between two people who loved each other. How could he possibly think a marriage between them would work? They barely knew each other. 'Loukas, it's terrible what happened to that poor girl—shocking and awfully sad. But you're not your father, and shouldn't be judged by his standards or lack thereof.'

'Try telling the media that.'

Emily sat quietly for the rest of the journey back to her flat. Loukas seemed disinclined to talk and she could hardly blame him. In the space of the evening, he had found out he was to become a father, had had to deal with her cutting her finger and fainting and take her to hospital and deal with an inquisitive public and hospital staff. She would discuss the marriage thing when they had both had a decent night's sleep and were in a better frame of mind.

But, when Loukas turned the corner to the townhouse her little flat was housed in, she realised the night wasn't over yet. Loukas slowed down to swing into the parking space two spots behind her car. 'Are you expecting visitors?' he asked.

'No.' Emily shrank back down in the seat as a man wielding a camera came rushing towards the car. A woman with a recording device was close behind. Another person hopped out of a car further along the street and came towards Loukas's side with a camera poised. Emily sent Loukas a panicked glance. 'How did they find me?'

'Someone must have tipped them off at the hospital,' Loukas said. 'Let me handle it.' He wound down his driver's side window to the approaching journalist.

The man leaned down. 'Mr Kyprianos, a source

tells us you and Miss Seymour are engaged and expecting a baby. Do you have any comment to make?'

'Only to say we're thrilled to be getting married and starting a family,' Loukas said. 'Now, if you'll excuse us, we have things to do.'

He got out of the car and came around to Emily's side, but the female journalist was already at the passenger window. 'Miss Seymour, how does it feel to be engaged to one of Greece's most eligible bachelors?'

Emily got out of the car and slipped her hand into Loukas's. 'It's…great. Wonderful. Amazing. I mean, *he's* amazing. Truly amazing and so kind and thoughtful and…'

Loukas's arm went around Emily's waist, drawing her close to his side. 'That's it, everyone. Emily's had a big day. So if you'll excuse—'

'What happened to your hand, Emily?' the same journalist asked.

'I—I broke a perfume bottle and cut my finger.'

'What does your father think of becoming a grandfather, Loukas?' one of the other journalists asked. 'Have you told him yet?'

'No, but I'm sure you'll take care of that for me,' Loukas said with an on-off movement of his lips. He led Emily to her front door and gestured for her to hand him the key. She rummaged in her purse, handed the key to him and Loukas unlocked the door and led her inside.

'How quickly can you pack a bag?' he asked once they were safely inside with the door closed.

Emily looked at him blankly. 'A bag? What for?'

'I'm taking you back to my hotel,' he said. 'It will be safer than here until this blows over.'

'So much for patient confidentiality,' she muttered, not quite under her breath.

'It wouldn't have been Dr Freeman. As you pointed out, it could've been anyone at the hospital. My money is on those two women. They probably got your address off the form you filled in.'

Emily folded her arms, casting him a look that would have done a jealous wife proud. 'If Dr Freeman hadn't got called away that night would you have slept with her?'

He gave her an unreadable glance. 'Maybe. Maybe not.'

'She was up for it,' she said. 'In fact, if you hadn't told her we were engaged, I reckon she would have asked for your number to hook up with you after work. You could be with her right now, having smoking-hot sex, instead of stuck here with—'

'Emily.' There was a strong note of calm reproof in his tone.

Emily was close to tears and spun away from him to pull the curtains across the windows to block the paparazzi from seeing inside her flat. Her life was spinning out of control. How could this be happening? One day she was anonymous, the next she was being hunted down like a famous celebrity. When would it stop? *Would* it stop?

'I reckon she's wondering how on earth you could have chosen me over her. I bet those journalists out there are wondering it too. And so will everyone who reads tomorrow's gossip. A man like you choosing a boring, unsophisticated legal secretary from Tottenham over an emergency doctor from Knightsbridge? What a joke.'

He came up close and turned her to face him, flinching when he saw her shimmering eyes. He lifted a hand to her face and gently tucked a strand of hair behind her ear, brushing away a couple of tears from the side of her left eye. 'Please don't cry.'

'I—I'm not c-crying.' Emily sniffed.

Loukas handed her a clean handkerchief that smelled of his aftershave and was warm from being housed close to his body. She buried her head in its citrus scented folds and allowed herself a couple of noisy sobs. One of his hands went to the back of her head and moved in slow, soothing strokes from the top of her scalp to the base of her neck, sending shudders of reaction through her body. Then he lifted her hair and brought his hand against the nape of her neck, his fingers warm and gentle as they moved through the fine hairs there, sending delicious currents of electricity to the core of her being.

When had anyone ever comforted her like this? Daniel had never been the cuddle-and-comfort type, which was understandable, now she knew how awkward it had made him feel. But even her mother wasn't great at affection. The best she got from her mother was an air kiss and a hug that lasted no longer than a blink. When had anyone ever just sat with her and held her? Loukas's hug made her feel safe and protected from the crazy world outside.

Emily slowly lifted her head out of the handkerchief and focussed her gaze on his dark inscrutable one. She bit her lower lip. 'Hormones. Sorry.'

A ghost of a smile flickered at one side of his mouth and his hand moved to cradle her cheek, his thumb stroking back and forth in a barely touching movement that set her facial nerves dancing. His eyes became hooded and he slipped his gaze to her mouth, lingering there for an infinitesimal moment. Emily sent the tip of her tongue out over her lips in a darting movement, unable to stop the impulse even though she knew it was a primary signal of arousal.

The air tightened. Crackling with possibilities. Erotic possibilities that made her blood tick and her heart trip.

His thumb moved to her bottom lip, stroking along it like someone smoothing out a tiny crease in silk. It was as if every nerve in her lip rose to the surface, swelling, pulsing, heating against the pad of his thumb. 'You have the most beautiful mouth.' Loukas's voice was so deep it sounded as though it had come from beneath the floor.

Emily touched his face with her uninjured hand, losing herself in the depths of his deep-brown gaze with its fringe of inky lashes. His eyes were so dark she couldn't tell where his pupils began and ended. 'What are we doing, Loukas?' Her voice was not much more than a whisper.

His warm breath wafted over her lips. 'This is what we're doing.' And his mouth came down on hers.

His lips moved with sensual expertise over her mouth, rediscovering its contours, drawing from her a response that made her blood sing in her veins.

Emily's hands crept up his chest and then linked around his neck, her body pressing closer to the warm, hard heat of his. His tongue stroked over the seam of her mouth and she opened to him on a sigh of pleasure. The glide of his tongue was just as intoxicating as the first time he'd kissed her. It sent every female hormone in her body into paroxysms of excitement. His tongue found hers and cajoled it into play, teasing it, stroking it, chasing it. Seducing it. Loukas's hands settled on her hips, holding her close to his body, where his blood pumped and his flesh surged. She moved against him instinctively, driven by primal urges she had no control over. He angled his head to deepen the kiss, one of his hands coming up from her waist to cup the side of her face, his fingers splaying through her hair.

He nudged against her lips and then nibbled the lower one until she was whimpering against his mouth. She sent her hands through the thick silk of his hair, tugging and releasing the slight curls, delighting in the way he made deep, guttural sounds of approval.

One of his hands went to her breast but their hormone-induced sensitivity sent her jerking back from him. 'Ouch!'

He looked down at her, frowning in concern. 'Did I hurt you?'

She winced. 'My breasts are really tender. It's the hormones.'

His hands settled back on her waist as gently as if she were made of gossamer. 'I'm sorry. I didn't realise. Are you okay?'

'I'm fine...'

Loukas stepped back from her with a rueful grimace. 'It's probably a good time to stop before things get out of hand.' He rubbed a hand over his face as if trying to recalibrate himself. 'This is turning out to be one hell of a night.'

Tell me about it.

Emily watched as he moved across to the window to check the street outside. 'Are they still there?'

He let the curtain drop back into place. 'No, but I still think you should come back to my hotel with me.'

'Surely that's not necessary?'

Something about his expression made her realise once he made up his mind it would not be changed without a fight. Even *with* a fight. 'Humour me, Emily. I know what the press are like. They'll be here first thing and hounding you for an exclusive.'

'I won't speak to them so—'

'You won't be able to help yourself.' His mouth had a wry slant to it. 'You'd be too worried about being rude. Before you know it, you'll be inviting them in for coffee and home-baked cookies and telling them your life story.'

Emily pressed her lips together, not sure she cared for his summation of her character. So she had a loose tongue at times? So what if she over-shared occasionally? It was only when she was nervous. And how did he know she had home-baked cookies in the house? He was making her out to be some sort of nineteen-fifties throwback, complete with frilled pinafore and polka-dotted headscarf. 'I'm not going to be able to avoid them for ever. I can't stay at your hotel indefinitely. You're only here for a week in any case.'

He looked at her for a long moment.

'Why are you looking at me like that?' she asked.

'I want you to come back to Corfu with me.'

Her stomach dropped like an anchor. 'What?'

'Just until the press interest dies down,' he said. 'My villa is secure from media intrusion. You can rest up without the constant threat of having a camera or microphone thrust in your face. We can stay there until the ceremony.'

Emily turned away, holding her arms across her middle. 'Now you're being ridiculous again.'

He came up behind her and turned her to face him, his hold gentle but firm—a bracelet of warm male fingers overlapping on her wrist, reminding her of his superior strength and essential maleness. His eyes held hers prisoner. 'I'm trying to protect you, Emily.'

The thought of someone offering to protect her

was tempting. Way more tempting than it should be for an emancipated woman of nearly thirty. But for so long Emily had craved security and stability. Would Loukas be that go-to person she'd thought she had in Daniel? The person who would stand up *for* her as well as *by* her? She allowed her mind to drift with the possibility of marrying him. She wouldn't have to be a single mum. She wouldn't have to worry about bringing up a baby alone. Loukas would be there as back-up, involved with the baby and always on hand if she needed extra support. She would be part of a family unit: mum, dad and baby. A unit of stability and belonging that she had longed for since she was a little girl.

You're thinking of marrying him? You took longer to choose that dress you're wearing.

But I like the thought of being protected.

You definitely need protecting—from your traitorous hormones, that's what.

If Emily went anywhere with Loukas who knew what might happen? One kiss a month ago and she'd ended up pregnant. A week or two at his private villa was just asking for trouble. She tried to ease out of his hold but his fingers countered the move by gently tightening. 'I can protect myself.' Somehow her voice didn't come out as stridently as she'd hoped.

One of his dark brows rose in a sceptical arc and he glanced pointedly at her bandaged finger. 'How's that working out for you so far?'

Clearly not well.

Emily compressed her lips again, shooting him a glare cold enough to freeze vodka. 'I can't just walk out on my job without notice.'

'Allegra's your boss, right? She'll understand. In fact, she'll encourage you to get away somewhere safe.'

Emily frowned. 'But what am I going to say to her?'

'Does she know about the pregnancy?'

'Not officially—I only told her I was late. You're the first person I've told.'

Something moved through his gaze, softening it. Darkening it. 'Thank you.'

'You're welcome.'

'You'd better call Allegra before she reads about us over breakfast,' Loukas said.

'Are you going to call Draco?'

He released her hand and stepped back from her. 'It's not something I've been looking forward to.'

'I can imagine it must be galling for you to admit to having knocked up the bridesmaid.' Emily's voice was so tart it was as if she were speaking through a mouthful of lemons. 'Especially since she's not your type.'

He shifted his lips from side to side as if monitoring his response. 'Someone's done an excellent job on your self-esteem.'

She sent him her best nose-in-the-air, haughty look. 'I'd like you to leave.'

'I'm not leaving without you,' he said with an intractable set to his features. 'Now, go and pack a bag, otherwise I'll pack it for you.'

Emily planted her feet, pushed her chin up higher and folded her arms. 'You're not the boss of me.'

You're not the boss of me? What are you? Six?
He's not telling me what to do.
Yes, he is, and by the look on his face you'd better do it.

Loukas held her gaze in a silent tug-of-war that did strange, fizzy things to the backs of her knees, like someone was trickling sand down her legs. Emily would have stuck it out to show she wasn't a pushover but a wave of nausea rose in her throat and she threw a hand over her mouth and made a mad dash to the bathroom.

She heard him come in behind her but she was beyond caring about having an audience to her wretchedness. Right then and there, an entire football stadium of fans could have crammed in and she wouldn't have cared. She flushed the toilet and dragged herself upright but Loukas already had a face cloth rinsed and ready for her. 'Here you go.'

She covered her clammy face with the cloth and then washed her face at the basin. She was acutely, intensely aware of him. Her bathroom was already on the phone-box-size side, but with him in there with her it shrank to the size of a tissue box.

Loukas placed his hands on the tops of her shoulders from behind, his hips close to her butt cheeks. If she moved half an inch she would come into intimate contact with him. The temptation to lean back into his fortress-like body was nothing short of overwhelming. She gripped the edge of the basin to stop herself from doing it. She met his gaze in the mirror and a jolt of something sharp and electric shot through her system. His hips brushed her from behind.

Oh, God. Oh, God. Oh, God.

How could she be thinking about sex when a minute ago she'd been yodelling over the toilet?

'Let me take care of you, Emily.' His voice had a note of determination. The note that made her want to forget all about female emancipation, park herself behind a picket fence and don a pinafore and oven mitts.

Emily turned to face him, her teeth sinking into her lower lip. 'Corfu does sound kind of nice...'

He tipped up her chin and for the first time she saw a glimmer of a smile tugging up the corners of his mouth. 'That's my girl.'

CHAPTER FOUR

LOUKAS WAS STAYING in Chelsea at one of the hotels
Emily had never expected to go into for a drink, let
alone stay the night in. Uniformed attendants with
top hats greeted them when Loukas pulled into the
bay in front of the stately entrance. The car doors
were opened and she stepped out on to the strip of
red carpet that led into the dazzling foyer. Her bag
was whisked away and Loukas took her arm and
looped it through his. 'We'll leave for Corfu after
lunch tomorrow. I have a couple of things to see to
first thing, but you can rest up here until it's time
to head to the airport.'

Emily's eyes rounded to the size of dinner plates
when she stepped into the hotel. Corinthian col-
umns divided the foyer, sprouting out of a sea of
black-and-white tiles. A central crystal chandelier
hung from the impossibly high ceiling and other
glittering lights were placed strategically upon the

walls. An ornate gold-framed mirror the size of her bedroom hung above a marble fireplace where some classic sofas and wing chairs were nestled to create a cosy setting.

On the other side of the room was a black grand piano, so glossy the chandelier above was reflected in its surface in dozens of sparkles that looked like scattered diamonds. White-columned archways divided the massive space into sections and the reception was at the far end where more uniformed staff were in attendance. Loukas informed them Emily would be joining him in his suite and then led her to the bank of lifts through another archway.

He held her hand while they waited for the lift, glancing down at her. 'How are you doing?'

Emily tried not to show how awestruck she was but she was pretty sure she was doing the kid-in-a-candy-store thing. Everywhere she looked was luxury beyond anything she had seen before. Even the lift call-button looked as though it was pure gold. 'I'm fine, but I could do with something to eat.'

'I'll order some room service for you.'

A short time later, Emily sat propped up with several cloud-soft pillows on the acre of bed. She had a silver service meal on a tray table parked over her stretched out legs. Loukas was seeing to emails on his smart phone and had so far not touched his own meal set on a table beside him. She picked at her dinner, not wanting to overdo things in case she had another attack of nausea. In between cautious mouthfuls, Emily took the time to study him while he was preoccupied with business. His forehead was creased in a frown of concentration, his shoulders hunched forward as he scrolled through his messages. Evening stubble surrounded his nose and mouth and flared either side of his jaw in a rich, dark swathe that made her itch to run her fingertips over it.

She remembered how that bristly skin felt against her smoother skin. After that night in his bed, it had taken days for the marks to fade from her face. And other more secret places. She'd had to use concealer to disguise it on her face and, every time she'd applied it, her stomach would free fall as she remembered the way the marks had got there.

Loukas glanced up from his phone to catch her looking at him. 'All done?'

Emily hoped she wasn't blushing but it sure felt like it. At this rate she could have moonlighted as a *bain-marie*. No dinner could ever go cold balanced on her cheeks. 'I'm done. Thanks, it was lovely.'

He rose from the chair and came over. When he

leaned down to lift the tray off the bed, Emily put her hand on one of his arms and met his dark gaze. 'You're being awfully good about all this… I mean, this must be your worst nightmare, and here you are waiting on me and looking after me like I'm some sort of princess.'

His eyes moved between each of hers, then he glanced down at her mouth. Loukas took a steadying breath, lifted the tray away and placed it on the table next to his untouched meal. He stood with his back to her and pushed a hand up his face and over the back of his hair but, rather than straightening it, it made it even more sexily tousled. He turned back around but his expression was impossible to read. 'You'd better get some sleep.'

'Where are you going to sleep?'

He nodded towards the sitting room next door. 'I'll take the sofa.'

Emily rolled her lips together and began to fiddle with the edge of the sheet. 'You don't have to do that. I mean, this bed is practically bigger than my flat.'

'Emily.' The way he said her name in that stern schoolmaster tone made her feel like a child who'd been told she wasn't allowed in the drawing room with the grown-ups.

She couldn't hold his gaze and focussed on

the hem of the sheet instead. 'Right, well, good-night, then.'

She saw his long trouser-clad legs appear beside the bed. He placed a gentle fingertip beneath her chin and elevated her gaze to meet his. 'I shouldn't have touched you in the first place,' he said. 'I was out of line. Way out of line.'

Emily couldn't peel her eyes away from the dark intensity of his. 'Why did you make the first move that night, after the wedding?'

His hand fell away from her face and he thrust both hands into the pockets of his trousers as if to keep them out of the way of temptation. 'I was... on edge.'

'On edge?' Emily asked. 'About what?'

'Stuff.'

'What stuff?'

He drew in a breath and released it in stages. 'Family stuff.'

'Your father?'

Something passed over Loukas's features, like a tide of tension stiffening his facial muscles in degrees until his entire face was a mask set in stone. 'That's enough talking for now. I'm keeping you up. You look done in. I'll see you in the morning.'

Emily frowned as the door closed behind him. She considered going after him to pump him for more information but the long day was finally catching up with her. She was almost too tired to remove her contacts and place them in the solution container she drew out of her bag beside the bed, but remove them she did. Then she sighed and leaned back against the downy-soft pillows and within seconds her eyes drifted closed...

Loukas gave up on sleeping on the sofa, even though it was reasonably comfortable. He sat staring sightlessly at the view from the windows, barely noticing the beads of rain dripping down the glass. He'd cancelled all but one of his work commitments so he could get Emily out of London and safely on Corfu, where hopefully they would be left in peace until he got a ring on her finger.

He hadn't yet given his mother or his sister the heads up about Emily. Not that he was in regular contact with them. He'd visited Ariana after her recent surgery, but mostly he kept his distance, because every time he phoned or visited he was conscious of how it reminded her of what he had done to her. He figured, out of sight, out of mind worked best for all of them. Ariana, thankfully, remembered nothing of the accident, and she accepted the years of operations and physical therapy with admirable if not downright astonishing fortitude.

But, even though they never talked of that day, it was something he could never forget. He had caused so much damage to his family, injuring his sister and destroying his mother's marriage as well. Her husband had left just over a year after the accident, unable to cope with his wife's absences while she helped Ariana in hospital and then the start of the long months in rehab.

Loukas had watched in despair as the people he loved most in the world had lost everything that was dear to them. His sister had lost her ability to run, play and dance, her future stolen from her, never to be regained. Her mother had lost the love she had found after her bitter divorce from his father and had become a shadow of herself, physically gaunt and emotionally fragile, only managing to survive out of her fierce determination to claw back her daughter from death's greedy jaws.

Their lives had improved a lot over the years— Loukas had seen to that, providing them with everything they needed—but at the end of the day it still came down to the painful reality that Ariana was never going to do all the things her peers took for granted. His mother was never going to get those lost years back and, because she was Ariana's full-time carer, there was no way she could have a life of her own.

And it was his fault.

How was he going to call his sister and mother to tell them about this new hurt he'd caused? He hated the thought of them opening a newspaper or news link and hearing about it that way, but how did you tell your family you'd got a girl you should never have slept with pregnant? Not that his mother would mind. If anyone was a frustrated grandmother it was she. He saw the way she looked longingly at passing prams and advertisements with babies and children in them. It was like a knife twisting in his gut to see how hard she tried to disguise it. But, because of his sister's on-going health issues, there would be no grandkids other than his.

Knowing he had taken away his sister's chance of becoming a mother made his guilt about the accident all the harder to bear. It was one of the reasons he had never planned to marry and have a family— because why should he have that privilege when his sister could not? Every milestone of his would be a guilt trip instead of a celebration.

Loukas got up from the sofa and crossed the suite to creak open the bedroom door. The light from the streetlights outside cast the bed in a beam of silver. Emily was curled up like a comma on the bed, barely taking up any space at all. Her brown-blonde hair was spread out over the pillow like a halo and her hand with its bandaged finger was tucked up near her chin, the other splayed on the sheet beside her head. She made a soft murmuring sound, rolled over and stretched like a cat, her small but perfect breasts rising under her top, the darker nipples showing through the fabric.

Emily suddenly opened her eyes and saw him standing there. She sat bolt-upright and reached for a pair of glasses beside the bed, pushed them up her nose and then grabbed at the sheet to pull it up to her chin. 'You gave me such a fright!'

'Sorry. I was just checking you were—'

'You could have knocked first.' Her mouth was just shy of a pout. 'How long have you been there?'

'Not long.'

She hugged her bent knees, giving him a look over the rim of her tortoiseshell glasses that reminded him of a child pretending to be a starchy librarian. 'How's the sofa working out for you?'

'Great.'

'Liar. I bet your legs hang over the edge.'

Loukas glanced at the bottle of contact lens solution beside the bed and the little container she housed them in. 'I didn't know you wore contacts. Were you wearing them the night we—'

'Yes, but I didn't take them out because…' Her

cheeks went a delicate shade of pink. 'I didn't have time.'

'We were in a bit of a hurry, weren't we?' He came to sit on the edge of the bed next to her bent legs. 'Can I get you anything? A drink?'

'No, I'm good.'

'Not sick?'

She lifted her good hand and crossed her middle finger over her index finger. 'So far, so good.' She uncrossed her fingers and then, after a brief moment, reached out to touch his jaw, her soft fingertips catching on his stubble. Her eyes behind the glasses looked big and luminous, her mouth so soft and kissable he had to pinch his lips together to stop himself from leaning forward to kiss her. 'I had beard rash for four days after that night we slept together. It cost me a fortune in concealer.'

As she dropped her hand, Loukas lifted his own and traced a fingertip down the creamy slope of her cheek all the way to her mouth. He slowly circled its Cupid's bow contours, watching as her lips trembled and quivered in response to his touch. 'Kissing you was my first mistake.'

Her pupils flared into dark pools of ink. 'Your second?'

'I'm about to make it right about now.' He brought his mouth down to hers and tasted her lips. Once. Twice. Three times. She gave a soft, breathless sigh and he touched down again, lingering longer this time, feeling the suppleness of her mouth melding against his, making the blood thunder through his body and charge south to his groin. He had never tasted a mouth as sweet as hers. Sweet and yet smoking hot. Heat exploded from her mouth to his, lighting fires all over his flesh, making him gather her closer, desperate to feel her body against his.

She wound her arms around his neck, her fingers playing with the ends of his hair, her soft mouth torturing his self-control.

What self-control?

Did he have any when it came to her? Every time he put his mouth on hers his willpower took leave without pay. Her little whimpers of encouragement made it impossible to pull back from her temptation. He deepened the kiss, exploring every corner of her mouth, enticing her tongue to play, flirt and mate with his. Loukas cupped her face in his hands, angling his head to gain better access, relishing the scent and texture of her skin.

Her fingers were on his scalp, massaging him into a stupor. Her touch unhinged him, unloosed in him a primitive urge to lose himself in her like he had done with no one else before. He always kept control. Always. But, with her mouth fused to his and her hands moving over him, his need for her was almost frightening.

He pulled back from her but kept his hands cradling her face. 'You are a dangerous young woman.'

Emily's toffee-brown eyes were guileless and she quickly straightened her crooked frames with her finger. 'Why?'

Loukas brushed the pad of his thumb over her kiss-swollen bottom lip. 'Because I can't seem to keep my hands off you no matter how much I tell myself to.'

Her hand came to rest on one of his wrists, her fingertips light as fairy feet. 'I have the same problem.' She moved her fingers to his mouth, circling it as he had done hers. 'Should we be doing this?'

'This?' Who was he kidding? He knew exactly what *this* was. *This* was magic. *This* was irresistible. *This* was the only thing he could think about. The only thing he wanted.

She leaned forward and pressed a feather-soft kiss to his mouth. 'Touching and kissing and... stuff.'

'Isn't that what engaged couples do?'

Her hand fell away from his wrist and her teeth began to work at her lower lip. 'I waited seven years for my ex to propose and he never got around to it. I only met you a month ago and you never *stop* mentioning marriage. When are you going to take no for an answer?'

He kept his gaze trained on hers. 'We can't retract our statement now without looking like fools. We don't have to be married for ever. Just long enough to get the press off our backs. I'm not offering you the fairy-tale. Just a convenient arrangement so that our child gets a good start in life. After that, we'll reassess if things aren't working out.'

Doubt flickered on Emily's face and her eyes became downcast. 'I don't know... It seems weird to be marrying someone I hadn't even met a month ago.'

'You will never want for anything. I will make sure of that.'

Twin pleats of worry divided her smooth brow. 'It's not about the money. We're not in love with each other.'

'Neither were Draco and Allegra but that seems to have turned out all right.'

'But Allegra was always a little bit in love with him,' she said. 'We, on the other hand, are practically strangers. I hardly know anything about you and you expect me to marry you?'

'This is the only way forward. We should get

married as soon as possible and then the press attention will go away, just like it did with Draco and Allegra.'

She narrowed her gaze. 'You'd seriously get married to a stranger just to stop a little press attention? *Really?*'

'We're doing this for our child, Emily. Why wait? Do you want to be hounded for the next eight months, having cameras and phones and recording devices thrust in your face every time you step out the door? Strangers taking photos of you while you're eating in cafés or restaurants or simply walking down the street? No. I didn't think so. We'll marry quickly and quietly and that will be the end of it. Problem solved.'

Something passed over Emily's face—a flash of panic followed by resignation. 'Okay, we'll do it your way. I'll marry you.' Her teeth kept going back to her lower lip. 'How soon were you thinking of—' she gave a tiny gulp '—doing it?'

'The end of the month.'

Her eyes widened. 'But that's only two weeks away!'

'So? It shouldn't take too much time to plan a simple ceremony with a handful of witnesses.'

'But won't people expect someone of your status and wealth to have a big church wedding?'

'I don't do things just because people expect me to,' Loukas said.

'No?' One of her brows rose in a wry you-can't-fool-me arc. 'Only marry a perfect stranger so people won't compare you to your father? Sure, I believe you.'

He pressed his lips together for a moment, determined not to be triggered by her little dig. It wasn't just about being compared to his father. He genuinely wanted to protect Emily and this was the only way he could see to do it. 'Do you *want* a big wedding?'

She gave an offhand shrug of one slim shoulder. 'Not particularly.'

'If you and your ex had married, what would the wedding have been like?'

Emily folded her arms and sent him a resentful glare. 'Could we talk about something else apart from my disastrous relationship with my ex?'

'Were you in love with him?'

Her gaze slipped out of reach of his. After a moment she released a short puff of a breath. 'I thought so, but I realised later I wasn't. Not the way other people describe being in love. I think I was in love with the idea of being in a relationship. Being a couple. Of having a base to come home to—of belonging to someone.'

'It's an easy mistake to make.'

Her eyes came back to his. 'Have you ever been in love?'

'No.'

'Never?'

'Never.'

She searched his gaze some more. 'Not even a teensy-weensy bit?'

'No.'

Her frown deepened. 'So you just sleep with women for the sex? You don't actually feel anything for them but pure and simple lust? Doesn't that seem a little…shallow?'

'No.'

'Well, it does to me.'

'Are you saying you felt something for me other than lust that night?' Loukas asked, drilling his gaze into hers.

She blew out another gust of a breath, her slim shoulders going down. 'Okay, you win. Point taken.'

Loukas put a hand at her nape and brought her head forward to press a soft kiss to the middle of her forehead. 'Go back to sleep, *glykia mou*. I'll see you in the morning.'

Emily lay staring at the ceiling once Loukas had left. So, she was going to marry him. Not that he'd given her much choice, but still. It wasn't exactly the most romantic proposal in the world: *we'll marry quickly and quietly and that will be the end of it.*

Sleep was out of the question, knowing he was in the next room tossing and turning on the sofa. Should she have asked him to stay? Asked him to make love to her?

What are you thinking?

I want him.

So? You had him and look what happened.

He wants me. I'm sure of it.

For sex, yes, but forget about anything else.

Emily didn't want anything else…did she? The marriage would be an arrangement, not a relationship in the truest sense. She wasn't in love with Loukas. This was a lust thing, and no doubt the pregnancy hormones were making it worse. His kiss had unravelled her. Again. As soon as his lips had touched hers she'd become a boneless, whimpering mess of need.

Emily turned over and hugged the nearest pillow but it was a poor substitute for his virile male body. But why hadn't he taken it further? Especially since he was so determined to marry her. Was he holding back from her until he got a ring on her finger? His ability to stop a kiss in its tracks made her self-doubts flash like warning lights. Daniel had always been able to pull away from a kiss. Always. It had made her feel undesirable, resistible. What if Loukas was only kissing her to keep her sweet about the marriage deal? What if he could resist her? *Would* resist her? Why was she signing up for such an arrangement? A marriage without love? A contract drawn up between two virtual strangers to live together until such time they didn't want to any more. How could she have agreed to that?

She'd had to because it wasn't just about what *she* wanted any more.

It was about what was best for their baby.

CHAPTER FIVE

THE NEXT MORNING Emily showered and changed into fresh clothes, and came out to the sitting room to find Loukas staring out of the rain-splattered windows with his hands in the pockets of the same trousers he had been wearing the night before, which were looking a little worse for wear. He must have heard her soft tread on the carpet as he turned to look at her. His features looked as tired as his trousers. 'How did you sleep?' he asked.

She glanced at the rumpled sofa. 'Probably a whole lot better than you.'

He acknowledged that with a wry quirk of his lips. 'The news of our engagement has gone viral.'

'Your mission is accomplished, then.'

He came over to her and took her gently by the upper arms, his gaze meshing with hers. 'I know this is a big step for you. It's a big step for me too. I never intended to marry anyone, but—'

'Why not?'

He released her from his hold and took a step back, his gaze shifting to avoid hers. 'It was never on my list of things to do.'

'You must have a reason why it's not on the list,' Emily said. 'Marriage hasn't exactly gone out of fashion. Most people aspire to settle down and raise a family at some stage of their life. Why not you?'

He pushed out his mouth on an expelled breath. 'My parents had a messy divorce.'

'So? That doesn't mean you would too.'

'True, but I preferred not to risk it.'

'So you'd rather spend your life drifting from one shallow hook-up to the next without really connecting on any level but the physical?'

'I've seen what it can do to kids when couples divorce,' he said. 'It's not pretty.'

'Is that what happened to you when your parents broke up?' Emily asked. 'You got caught in the crossfire?'

His expression gave little away and yet Emily sensed this was a difficult and painful subject for him. Maybe she'd picked up a bit of her mother's mind-reading ability after all.

Scary thought.

But then, she'd gleaned enough about his father to realise things might not have been too easy for

Loukas and his mother. 'Talk to me, Loukas,' she said softly. 'If we're going to get married then surely I should know a little bit about your background?'

He took a deep breath and then released it in a slow stream, as if he was letting go of something that had long been tied up tightly inside him. 'My parents divorced when I was six. I moved with my father to the States soon after. It wasn't a good experience. But then divorce rarely is for the kids involved.'

Emily frowned, thinking of him as a small boy travelling to new place, a new culture, without his mother. How had he coped with the separation? What little kid didn't want their mum at the ready? Why had his father got sole custody? 'Why with your father and not your mother?'

Loukas gave her a lopsided grimace. 'My father wanted to punish my mother for having the audacity to ask him for a divorce. He got an attack-dog lawyer to tear her reputation to pieces. After he was finished, there wasn't a court anywhere in Greece who would have awarded her custody of a stray dog, much less a child.'

'But that's awful! Your poor mum. And poor you. You must've been distraught to be separated from her so young.'

The taut line about his mouth made her wonder

if he had ever forgiven his father. 'My father soon lost interest in bringing up a small child. I spent time with a number of nannies before I was packed off to boarding school in England. And it wasn't just because I was too young to go to an American boarding school. He didn't want me coming home for weekends and generally getting in the way.'

Emily decided she didn't like Loukas's father one little bit. His treatment of women was appalling. How could a man be so cruel as to separate a small boy from his mother, only to dump him in a boarding school thousands of miles away for the sake of convenience? No wonder Loukas wanted to do everything he could to avoid being compared to his father.

A marriage between Loukas and her didn't seem so outrageous now she understood a little more about his background. Of course he would want to do the best thing for his child, and protect and provide for the mother of his baby so he wouldn't be linked in any way to his father's shocking behaviour. 'Did you ever get to see your mother?'

'Once I was at boarding school I spent holidays with her. My father didn't seem to care about her having custody by then.'

'Did your mother ever remarry?'

Something passed over his face: a shadow in his

eyes, a tensing of muscles, his locked jaw. It was as if what he had released moments ago was now being reined back in and locked down tightly again. 'Yes, but it didn't work out.'

Emily knew lots of second marriages failed but she wondered if there was more to Loukas's mother's story than he was prepared to share. She sensed his guardedness whenever she touched on the subject of his family. But then, with a jerk of a father like his, no wonder he was a little reticent about talking about his family. 'Just because your parents and subsequent partners' relationships didn't work out doesn't mean you'll suffer the same curse,' she said. 'I haven't had the best role model in the world but it hasn't stopped me wanting the fairy-tale.'

Which you will be giving up if you marry him.

Don't remind me.

Just saying.

'The break-up of any relationship where feelings are involved is difficult.'

'Is that why you never do long-term relationships?'

'I hate hurting people,' he said. 'I see no point in giving someone false hope. I've made it a policy to be scrupulously honest about what I'm prepared to give.'

Which he had been with her that night. Brutally honest.

No-strings sex. No phone numbers. No follow-ups.

His words hadn't been all that important to her back then. All she had thought about was how his mouth felt on hers, how he made her body sing with delight when he made love to her. 'But how long do you think our marriage would last? Are you expecting it to—'

'I don't expect you to commit to me for life,' he said. 'That's why I don't see the point in making a show out of the wedding. But I think we should remain married for the sake of the baby for three or four years at the very least. It will give our child a secure base before they go to school.'

Three or four years. It wasn't exactly a lifetime. And she would be fully supported and the baby would have everything it needed. Besides, Emily found Loukas increasingly intriguing. He was like a secret code she wanted to solve. Was a short-term marriage a stupid move on her part or the best thing under the circumstances? 'So...you're not worried about marrying a virtual stranger?' she said.

'We might not know much about each other but we do know we have the right chemistry,' Loukas said.

But would it be enough? Emily wondered if she was being a fool even considering it, let alone accepting his proposal. She had longed for one from her ex for seven years, longed and prayed for it every single day, and it had never been forthcoming. Now she'd had a proposal from a man she was fiercely attracted to but hardly knew. And she was having his baby. 'I wish you'd given me a little more time to think about this...'

'What's to think about? Most girls would jump at the chance to marry a rich man.'

Emily lifted her chin. 'If you think I'd marry a man simply because he's rich then you're very much mistaken. I'm not a gold-digger. Your money doesn't mean anything to me. It certainly wasn't why I slept with you.'

'Wasn't it?' Something dark and cynical glinted in his gaze.

'No.'

'Then why did you sleep with me?'

Emily forced herself to hold his gaze. 'You kissed me, that's why.'

He closed the distance once more and traced the line of her jaw with an indolent fingertip, his eyes holding hers in a sensually charged lock. 'Do you sleep with every man who kisses you?'

'No.'

'So...' His fingertip traced the vermillion border of her lower lip, his body so close to hers she could feel the warmth of him, and smell the intoxicating citrus notes of his aftershave. 'If I kissed you right now would you sleep with me?'

Emily's lip was buzzing from his touch, her inner core already contracting at the thought of his hot male mouth coming down on hers. Her heart was racing so fast, if there'd been a cardiologist handy they would have sent for an immediate EEG. Or defibrillator paddles. What was it about this man that made her turn into a wanton woman with no measure of self-control? He only had to touch her and she trembled with need. 'But you don't want to sleep with me,' she said in a voice that sounded nothing like hers. It was too husky. Sexy husky. Phone-sex husky.

Loukas sent his fingertip over her top lip, making every nerve scream for him to replace it with his mouth. 'What makes you think that?'

'You didn't want to share the bed with me last night.'

His fingertip did another round of her mouth. 'I was concerned about you. You were sick, exhausted. It would have been insensitive of me.'

I'm not sick now.

Emily didn't say it out loud but her hands going

to the front of his chest communicated it anyway. She gazed into the depths of his eyes, her insides stretching, stirring with the same need she saw reflected there. She lowered her gaze to his mouth, studying its contours, the way his dark, urgent stubble surrounded it. Had she ever seen a more fascinating mouth? That mouth had pleasured every inch of her body, done things to her secret places no one had ever done before. Her body thrummed even now with the memory of it.

Loukas brought her chin up with his fingertip, his lower body brushing against hers pelvis to pelvis. 'I want you. You can't be in any doubt of it, surely?'

Emily felt the hard contour of his growing arousal, the surge of blood so similar to the way her body swelled and moistened in secret. 'I want you too.' Desperately. Feverishly.

His hands cradled her face, his fingers splaying through her hair, his mouth coming down to hers in a searing kiss that spoke of primal urgings of his body that echoed her own. His tongue entered her mouth in a slow, silky thrust that made her inner core pulse and pound with lust. Her hands slid further up his chest to encircle his neck, her fingers caressing the tousled curls that brushed his collar. He groaned and deepened the kiss, his tongue exploring the recesses of her mouth with increasing fervour. A hot fizz filled her core as he brought her closer to his body, one of his hands settling in the small of her back to keep her in place.

Emily kissed him with the same blistering passion, her tongue duelling and dancing with his in little flicks and darts that made him murmur deep sounds of approval, making her feel more of a woman than she had ever done before. Desire rose in her like a swirling current, moving through her flesh with unstoppable force.

Loukas left her mouth to kiss his way down her neck, lingering over the pleasure spots he'd discovered that night a month ago. He came just shy of her breasts, his hands cupping her ribcage below them. 'I don't want to hurt you.'

'I'll be fine if you don't squeeze them.'

He moved her top aside and brushed his lips over the upper curve of her left breast. Then he sent his tongue in a rasping lick down the valley between her breasts. Well, maybe 'a valley' was stretching it a bit. Her pregnancy hormones had a little catching up to do, but she lived in hope. 'Tell me if I'm being too rough.'

Emily was fast moving beyond speech. She was having enough trouble breathing as it was. His tongue moved over the top side of her right breast before he unclipped her bra and stroked each of her nipples with his tongue. He kissed his way back up to her mouth, subjecting it to a long, slow kiss that fuelled her desire to a point where she was whimpering.

Emily could barely recall the steps of how she got there, but somehow she was lying on her back on the bed and Loukas was kissing his way down past her belly button to the triangle of cotton she was wearing. Yes, white, boring cotton. Why wasn't she wearing sexy black, cobwebby knickers?

He peeled the cotton down and gently traced the seam of her body with his tongue. The sensations tingled through her flesh, her nerve fibres shuddering as the strokes increased in pressure and intensity when he encountered the most swollen, tender part of her. She sucked in a sharp breath as the tension in her body gathered to one point as the wave approached. It seemed he knew her body better than she knew it herself. Within seconds she was convulsing with an orgasm that left her not just shaken and stirred but with her senses reeling.

But, just when she thought he was going to take things a step further for his own pleasure, he gave her a rueful grimace and stood, stepping away from the bed. 'Maybe we should save this until I have more time,' he said. 'I have a meeting in half an hour and I don't want to rush this.'

Emily wondered if it was the time factor or whether he didn't fancy her half as much as she'd thought. There had been no hesitation that night a month ago. No pulling away from kisses, no half measures of pleasuring. It had been full-on I-want-you-right-now sex. She'd got off. He'd got off. Or they'd got off together. Had she imagined how good it had been that night a month ago? Had the glasses of champagne she'd had that night blurred her memory?

Or was he a bit squeamish about her pregnancy? Some men found it a turn-on; others found it confronting to make love to a pregnant woman, worried they might hurt the baby or something. She pulled her knickers and top back into place, bundling her bra into one hand. 'I guess you've proved your point.'

Loukas frowned. 'What do you mean?'

'I have zero self-control around you.'

He grazed her cheek with his fingertip. 'Will you be all right here on your own? Don't leave the suite. Call room service if you need anything. I won't be long—two hours, tops. It's a meeting with a government security agency and people have flown in from all over the country for it. I couldn't cancel it at short notice.'

'I'll be fine.'

'Do you want me to call Allegra for you, to tell her you won't be in for a few days?'

'No. I'll do it. I'm surprised she hasn't already called to ask me what's going on. But she's in the process of moving her practice to Greece, so is probably a bit distracted just now and hasn't seen the newsfeed yet.'

He bent down and brushed her hair back from her forehead. 'Be good while I'm away.'

Emily had barely straightened her clothes and hair when she heard her phone ringing from where it was plugged into a charger next to the bed. She knew it was her mother because she had set her number to ring with a particular ringtone. 'Mum, I was going to call—'

'Why am I the last person to know my one and only daughter is engaged and having a baby? What on earth is going on? I didn't even know you were dating someone.'

'I'm sorry, but it's all happened so quickly, I didn't have time to—'

'I hope you've established if he's gay or not,' her mother said.

'He's definitely not gay.' Emily placed a hand on her still flat tummy. It seemed unbelievable to think a tiny embryo was growing inside her womb, a combination of Loukas's DNA and hers making a little person who would, in a few months' time, be in her arms.

'Anyway, I knew you were pregnant well before I saw it splashed all over social media this morning,' her mother said.

Emily didn't really believe her mother could read minds, auras or tealeaves, but who knew what maternal sixth sense was at work? Not that their mother-daughter bond was particularly strong or anything. It was currently running on about two bars of signal strength. 'How could you have possibly known I was pregnant?'

'You haven't had PMS this last month. You always get crabby with me when you're due. Crabbier than usual, I mean.'

'That might've been because I took that vile-tasting liquid supplement you gave me.'

Her mother gave a snort. 'You haven't taken any of it. I checked the bottle last time I was over at your place.'

Emily had always thought her mother had missed her calling as a forensic detective. Which was why she'd been avoiding her until she'd told Loukas about the baby. Her mother would have ferreted out that stash of pregnancy tests like a sniffer dog on a drug bust. 'I'm hopeless at remembering to take medication—you know that.'

'Clearly you've neglected to take your contraceptive pill. How far along are you?'

She let out a jagged breath. 'I wasn't on the pill— I was taking a break after all those years on it. I'm four weeks or thereabouts.'

'You didn't think about terminating?'

'No.' It shocked Emily that it hadn't been the easiest decision to make. She'd always thought she would be thrilled about one day falling pregnant. But when she'd missed her period the panic had consumed any sense of thrill. The doubts and worries had rained on her like arrows: how would she cope with a baby? What if Loukas didn't want to have anything to do with their child? What if he hated her for keeping it? Or, worse, hated the child? She had worked at a law firm long enough to know there were men out there who began to hate their children because they'd been conceived with a partner they now detested.

It wasn't the way she had pictured her life panning out. She had pictured a white wedding to a man she loved and who loved her back, and then raising a family with him, a dream family, as she had longed for during her peripatetic childhood.

'Well, having a kid is one thing, but marrying the guy is another,' her mother said. 'Who marries because of a baby these days? It wasn't mandatory even in my day.'

All the same, it would have been nice to find out the guy's name, even if you didn't end up marrying him.

Emily didn't say it out loud because every time she said anything about her mother's casual approach to sex she ended up sounding like a nineteen-fifties Sunday School teacher. 'I want my baby to have a father in its life.'

'I know you think you've missed out on having a father but not every man is cut out to be a dad,' her mother said. 'Some men can't cope with the responsibility.'

Nor can some mothers.

Emily sometimes felt her mum didn't enjoy being a mum and had only given birth to her so she could tick the box marked 'Mother'. Her approach to motherhood was the same as her approach to everything else. She would do it with great passion for a period of time and then the novelty would wear off and she would abandon it to sign up for something else that had seized her interest. Emily had barely been out of nappies when her mother had started offloading her to other people whenever she could to go on yet another yoga, mind or body retreat. Most of her school holidays had been spent in holiday care because her mother had always had better things to do than hang out with her.

'Why are you marrying this man?' her mother asked. 'Do you love him?'

Emily had no choice but to lie. She couldn't tell her mother the truth. She would never hear the end of it. 'Of course I love him.'

'You said you were in love with Daniel and look how that turned out,' her mother said. 'I told you he was hiding something the first time I met him. He gave off a furtive vibe. You wasted years on him. Years and years and years.'

Don't remind me.

'Look, I really have to go now, as—'

'You always do that,' her mother said. 'You run away from stuff that cuts too close to the bone. That's why you stayed with Daniel so long. You refused to face up to what was staring you in the face. If you'd listened to me from the get-go, you would've saved yourself a heap of heartache. His chakras were blocked. I knew it from the first time I met him but did you listen to me? No.'

'I'm marrying Loukas, Mum, okay? We're in love and can't wait to be a family.'

'When do I get to meet him?' her mother asked. 'I'll do a chart for him. What's his birth date?'

Emily mentally gulped. 'Erm…'

Her mother made a sound that had a broad hint of 'got you' about it. 'You don't know, do you? How well do you know this man if you don't even know when his birthday is?'

'I do know him,' Emily said. 'I know enough about him to know he's a good man who'll stand by the baby and me no matter what.'

'He's pretty wealthy according to the press,' her mother said. 'Funny, but I never took you for a gold-digger. You didn't trap him, did you?'

'How can you even *think* that?' Emily asked. 'Surely you know me better than that?'

Her mother gave a long-winded sigh. 'Sometimes I wonder if I know you at all, Emily Grace.'

Likewise.

'Look, I have to go—I'll talk to you some other time. Bye.' Emily clicked off the phone and then turned it to silent in case her mother called back and began another lecture. She sat on the edge of the bed and took a few seconds to calm herself. Not an easy task after a conversation with her mother.

Not an easy task, period.

* * *

Emily picked up her phone to call Allegra but then decided she would go in to see her at the office instead. Loukas had told her not to leave the suite, but surely she could dash out to see Allegra, who was coming in that morning after spending a few days with Draco on his private island in Greece? Besides, who would recognise her without Loukas by her side? He was the one who was the press magnet, not her. She could nip to the office and back and no one would even notice.

Emily slipped out of a side entrance of the hotel and jumped in a cab, arriving at the office a short time later. When Allegra saw her she signalled for Emily to come into her office out of the hearing of the junior staff. She closed the door and came over to where Emily was standing. 'I've been calling for the last hour but you haven't answered. What's going on?'

Emily had forgotten she'd turned her phone to silent after she'd spoken with her mother. 'Well, firstly the test was positive. All seven of them were.'

'Oh, Em. I don't know what to say. Congratulations?'

'Congratulations twice over,' Emily said. 'I suppose you've read the news about us being engaged?'

'I did, and you could have knocked me down

with a finch's feather,' Allegra said. 'He actually *asked* you to marry him?'

'*Told* me would be more appropriate,' Emily said with more than a touch of wryness. 'I thought you said he was dead set against marriage? I swear to God, if there had been a priest or an Elvis impersonator handy Loukas would've demanded he marry us on the spot.'

'But is that what you want?' Allegra asked. 'I mean, you only met him a month ago. Are you sure you're doing the right thing? You hardly know each other.'

'I'm not at all sure; in fact I've never felt more confused in my entire life. But I want my baby to have a father and Loukas wants to be involved. He's worried about everyone thinking he'll be like his waste-of-space father. Did you know what a jerk his dad is?'

'Draco mentioned something about a scandal with a girl Loukas's father got pregnant but he didn't discuss it in too much detail,' Allegra said. 'Apparently Loukas doesn't like too many people knowing about it.'

'Can't say I blame him,' Emily said. 'Loukas wants me to fly to Corfu with him today. I know it's hideously short notice, but can you spare me for a couple of weeks?'

'Of course, but I'm worried about you rushing into this. You've barely had time to get used to the idea of being pregnant and now you're talking about marriage.'

'Yes, well, you can blame the press for that,' Emily said. 'We were at the hospital last night—'

'The hospital?' Allegra suddenly noticed Emily's bandaged finger. 'What happened to your finger?'

'Long story.'

'Tell me.'

'I was working up the courage to tell Loukas about the baby when I broke—'

'So he came to see you? In person?'

'Yes. He finally called. I didn't think it was right to tell him over the phone, so when he came round to take me out to dinner—'

'He asked you out to dinner?' Allegra asked, eyes wide. 'Before he knew anything about the baby?'

'Yes.'

'I can't wait to tell Draco. Why did he call you?'

'He wanted to see me again. He was only offering me a fling, mind you. Nothing permanent. But when I knocked over the bin and he saw all the pregnancy tests—'

'You mean you didn't actually tell him? He found out by default?'

Emily bit her lip. 'I know, I know, I know. I'm the world's biggest coward. I was trying to tell him but couldn't quite work up the courage.'

Allegra pulled out the chair for Emily to sit on and then, once Emily was seated, she perched on the edge of her desk, facing her. 'You don't have to marry him if you don't want to, Em.'

'Funny, but I seem to remember me saying something similar to you not that long ago,' Emily said with a pointed look.

Allegra did a self-effacing little eye-roll. 'Yes, well, I'm lucky it all worked out in the end.' Her frown snapped back. 'But Loukas isn't Draco. Draco told me no one gets close to Loukas. Think about it, sweetie. You're an open book, but he's as tight as a bank vault in a recession. Are you sure you'd feel comfortable marrying someone like that?'

Emily averted her gaze to focus on her hands resting on her thighs. 'I know he's a little locked down, but I'm just starting to peel back his layers. He's my baby's father and he wants to marry me, and with everything else that's been going on I can't see how I can say no now. I don't want him to be compared to his father.'

She looked back up at Allegra. 'I want people to see the Loukas I see. The one Draco knows as his best friend. He's a good man, a decent and honourable man. I want to get closer to him, and marrying him would be a good way to do it. Does that make sense?'

Allegra leaned down to press one of her hands on Emily's, her gaze warm with concern. 'Are you in love with him?'

Emily did her bunny-rabbit twitch, a habit she'd had since childhood when she'd first started wearing glasses and had to winch them back up her nose. She wore contacts now but the habit remained. 'I like him, otherwise I wouldn't have slept with him. I'm not a one-night-stand person. But I'm not in love with him.'

But how long before you are?

I'm not going to fall in love with him.

Ha-de-ha-ha-ha.

Allegra gave her hand a little squeeze. 'I hope it works out for you, Em. I really do. But, just in case it doesn't, remember I'm always here for you. Whatever you decide to do.'

'Thing is, Loukas doesn't want a big wedding, so we're having a quiet ceremony to keep the press interest down.'

'Won't you be terribly disappointed?' Allegra asked, frowning again. 'You've been talking about weddings ever since you first came to work for me.

You were so excited about being my bridesmaid. Surely you want to have more than a civil ceremony?'

Emily shrugged to disguise her niggling sense of disappointment. She had been picturing her dream wedding since she was a small child. Being the only child of a single mother who was staunchly against the notion of marriage had had the opposite effect on her. But if she married Loukas that dream would have to be relinquished. One of many she would have to let go. 'A big wedding will take months to organise and by then I'll be showing. No, it's better this way.'

'What does your mother think of all this?'

Emily grimaced. 'I told her I was in love with Loukas.'

Allegra's brows lifted. 'Did you, now?'

'It was easier than explaining everything. She wanted to do an astrology chart for him but I didn't know his birthday. I felt like such an idiot.'

'Was she excited about being a granny?'

Emily snorted. 'Can you picture my mother knitting booties? One thing I do know. There's no way she'll want to be called Granny or Nanna. She'll want to be called Willow.'

Allegra's brow furrowed. 'I thought her name was Susannah?'

Emily gave her a welcome-to-the-crazy-world-of-my-mother look. 'She did a "Names and Their Influence on Your Success" workshop a couple of months back. Apparently Willow has a better vibe or something. I just count myself lucky she didn't do that workshop before naming me. I dread to think what she might have come up with instead of Emily Grace.'

Allegra gave a wistful smile. 'At least you still have her.'

Emily felt a jab of remorse for harping on about her wacky mother when Allegra had lost hers when she was twelve. Allegra's children would only have one grandfather, Allegra's father, to whom she wasn't all that close, as Draco had lost both his parents when he was young. 'Sorry. That was a bit insensitive of me.'

'It's fine,' Allegra said with a closed-mouth smile. 'My mother and I weren't all that close anyway. Have you got time for a coffee and a choc-chip muffin?'

Emily put her hand over her mouth and gulped. 'Ack! Don't mention food.'

CHAPTER SIX

LOUKAS GOT BACK to the hotel to find the suite empty. He went through every room, even going so far as to open the wardrobes, but there was no sign of Emily. He whipped out his phone and dialled her number but it went through to the message service. Panic gripped him by the throat, tightening his airway until he could barely snatch in a breath. Where was she? Was she ill? Had she been taken to hospital? Had she gone outside and been hounded by the press? Perhaps chased down the street? Got hit by a bus? Kidnapped? The list of possibilities rushed through his brain like a toxic fever. His heart hammered so hard it was as if a construction site were inside his chest.

He called the front desk, asking if anyone had seen his fiancée. He felt a fool for having to ask it. 'No, Mr Kyprianos,' the receptionist said. 'Perhaps she's gone shopping for the wedding. There are three bridal stores and two florists on this block. This area's very popular for brides-to-be.'

Loukas put down the phone and wiped the back of his hand over his clammy brow. He had to get a grip on himself. There was probably a perfectly good explanation for why Emily had disobeyed his instruction to stay in the suite. The sense of power-lessness was sickening, reminding him of the day of the accident when so many lives had careened out of control.

Why had Emily gone? Where had she gone? Was she coming back? Or had he scared her with his insistence on marriage? Sure, it was a big step to get married. He might not be perfect husband ma-terial but it wasn't as if he was some boorish oaf who wouldn't look after her. He tried her phone another time but it went to message service again. His hand tightened on the phone until he thought the screen would crack. Should he do a ring-around of the hospitals to see if she'd been admitted? Ask the hotel to run the CCTV tapes to see if she'd left the hotel with someone?

The door suddenly opened and Emily came in. 'Oh…you're back.'

Relief collided with anger that she'd put him through such a hellish few minutes. 'Where the hell were you?' Loukas asked. 'I've been out of my head with worry. I thought I told you to stay put until I got back?'

She slipped her bag off her shoulder and placed it on the table near the door, her movements slow and measured, as if she was frightened of setting off a loaded bomb. 'I went to work to arrange for some leave.'

'You could have phoned to do that.'

Her brown eyes contained a hint of defiance. 'I preferred to do it face to face. Allegra's my best friend. I wanted to explain what was going on between us in person.'

'What did she say?'

'She has some misgivings about us rushing into marriage.'

'That's rich, coming from her.'

'Yes, I said much the same thing,' she said. 'But at least she knew the man she was marrying.'

Loukas let out a long breath to bring down his crazy heartbeat. 'We'll get to know each other in time, Emily. This is an unusual situation and it calls for an unusual solution. Did the press follow you?'

'Nope, I went out a side entrance and caught a cab to work,' she said with an element of smugness in her voice. 'I came back in the same way.'

'You scared the hell out of me, disappearing like

that,' he said. 'Why didn't you leave a note or send me a text?'

She shifted her weight from foot to foot, like a child caught out in some misdemeanour. 'I thought I'd be back before you.'

'I would appreciate it if you would obey my instructions in future,' Loukas said. 'I didn't insist you stay here to punish you. I was genuinely concerned about you. The paparazzi can be ruthless in hunting down a target. You can get injured trying to escape.'

'As you can see, I'm perfectly fine and, just for the record, I'm not in the habit of taking orders from the men in my life,' she said with an uppity tilt of her chin.

'I'm the only man in your life from this moment. Understood?'

Twin pools of colour collected on her cheeks, either from embarrassment or anger, he couldn't quite tell. 'Am I the only woman in yours?' she asked.

'Yes.' Loukas was surprised at how good it felt to say it. Shocked, even. He normally found relationships claustrophobic but somehow being connected to Emily didn't feel like that. It felt like a discovery. An adventure. Every day he learned something new about her. 'I expect nothing less than absolute fidelity while we are together. Are you okay with that?'

'Yes, of course,' she said. 'I wouldn't agree to marry you if you didn't promise me that.'

'Fine.' He studied her for a moment. 'How are you feeling?'

'I was a bit queasy when I was with Allegra but I'm okay now.'

Loukas slipped his hand into his pocket. 'I bought this on the way back to the hotel after the meeting. I hope it fits.'

She took the designer ring-box from him and nudged it open. 'Oh, my goodness, it's gorgeous!'

He hadn't had much time to choose after the meeting, but he figured she wasn't the flashy big ring type. He'd gone for a more subtle design with a high-quality diamond and a classic setting that would enhance her small hand rather than swamp it. He took the ring from the velvet lining and slid it along her ring finger, privately pleased he'd got the size spot-on. 'Do you like it?'

Her toffee-brown eyes were shining so much they were dazzling. 'It's beautiful. But you shouldn't have spent so much money. What if I lose it? I'm hopeless with jewellery. I've lost three pearl earrings and a diamond stud in the last year.'

Loukas suppressed a smile. 'Don't worry. It's insured.'

She held the ring up to the light, turning it this

way and that. 'I'll be super-duper careful, I promise.'
She lowered her hand and gave him a smile. 'Thank
you, Loukas. It was awfully generous of you.'

Loukas thought her smile gave the diamond a
run for its money in terms of brilliance. He had
never seen a smile so engaging as hers. When the
edges of her mouth tipped up, two dimples appeared
in her cheeks. 'You're welcome.'

There was a little silence.

Emily brushed back a loose strand of hair from
her face. 'What time are we leaving?'

He wished he hadn't booked the lunchtime flight.
Right then, he could think of nothing he'd rather do
than spend the next couple of hours in that bed with
her to show her his self-control wasn't in as good
a shape as she thought. But he wanted to get out of
London, away from all the attention of the press.
'Our flight is at one p.m., which doesn't leave us
much time. Do you need a hand packing?'

'No. I'm all good.'

The flight to Corfu was direct from London and it
seemed no time at all before they arrived at Loukas's villa set on a hilltop overlooking the stunning
view of the ocean. The villa was Venetian-style
with formal gardens out the back leading to wood-
land filled with pines, Holm oaks and wild olives.

At the front of the villa was a sun-drenched flag-stone terrace with a swimming pool that beckoned to Emily in the shimmering heat of the late after-noon.

The housekeeper came out of the villa and greeted Emily with a wide smile, her hands clasped together, as if giving thanks to the divine being who had orchestrated her boss bringing home a bride-to-be. 'So happy to meet you, Dhespinis Emily,' she said after Loukas introduced them. 'I have waited a long time for this day. I was won-dering if it would ever come. And a baby too! It is a dream come true.'

Emily painted on a smile. 'Thank you. It is very nice to be here.'

The housekeeper beamed at Loukas. 'I have a lovely surprise for you.'

Loukas's tightly compressed expression gave the impression he didn't much care for surprises. 'Oh, really?'

Chrystanthe's expression, on the other hand, was not unlike that of a doting fairy godmother who had just waved her magic wand and pulled off the grand wish of the century. She kept looking from Loukas to Emily with a wide smile on her face and her black button eyes twinkling. 'Your mother and sister are here. They arrived half an hour ago. They're waiting in the drawing room.'

His sister? Since when had Loukas had a sister? Why hadn't he mentioned her? She'd thought he was an only child of divorced parents. He had only been six years old when his parents had broken up. He had never said anything about a sibling, either older or younger. Allegra hadn't mentioned anything about him having a sister, either, which made Emily wonder if even Draco knew about her existence.

If not, why not?

Emily glanced at Loukas to find him frowning darkly. 'That's…nice,' he said, but the way he hesitated over the word 'nice' suggested he considered it far from so.

'They came off the luxury cruise you sent them on because they heard the news of your engagement,' the housekeeper said. 'They said they wanted to congratulate you in person.'

'Right,' Loukas said, taking Emily's hand. 'We'd better go see them.'

Emily waited until the housekeeper had gone ahead before asking, 'Is there anything else I should know about you that you haven't yet told me? Why didn't you tell me you had a sister?'

'Half-sister.'

'That's beside the point. You gave me the impression you were an only child,' she said. 'What sort of fool will I look if I don't know everything there is to know about you? I don't even know when your birthday is.'

'December twenty-eighth.'

'Capricorn.' Emily rolled her eyes. 'I should have guessed. You climb to the top and let nothing get in your way of a goal. You have trouble expressing feelings and do rather than say—or so my mother will tell you. She's done a course.'

'When's yours?'

'March second—Pisces. Apparently I'm self-less to a fault, unassuming and naïve and deeply emotional. Go me.'

Loukas led Emily inside the villa's foyer. If she had thought the hotel last night was spectacular, then this more than topped it. It wasn't a showy, over-done expression of wealth, but rather an understated simplicity of design and décor that spoke of a man with good taste and an excellent eye for detail. The walls of the foyer were adorned with priceless works of art, the polished marble floors covered strategically here and there with ankle-deep Persian rugs, and a staircase with glossy black balustrading led to the upper levels.

He took her to the main sitting room where a collection of plush sofas in brocade the colour of milky coffee sat around a rug beneath a central crystal chandelier. Lamps sat on side tables, their muted light giving the vast room a cosy atmosphere. The walls were bone-white with soft green-grey wainscoting and feature trims that continued the Venetian theme.

A steel-grey-haired woman in her fifties rose from a wing chair near the marble fireplace and, to her left, a younger, frail-looking woman in her early twenties, presumably Loukas's sister, was sitting in a wheelchair with a light throw rug over her knees.

'Loukas,' his mother said without approaching him, her tentative expression giving every indication she wasn't sure of the reception she would receive. 'I hope you don't mind us dropping in without notice, but we were so delighted by your news, we couldn't stay away. We won't stay long. We don't want to be in the way, but we just wanted to meet Emily.'

'It's nice to see you both,' he said. 'This is Emily.' He brought her forward with a hand on the small of her back. 'Emily, this is my mother, Phyllida Ryan, and my half-sister, Ariana.'

'I'm delighted to meet you both,' Emily said, taking his mother's hand and then his sister's.

Ariana smiled shyly up at Emily. 'Loukas is such a dark horse. He never tells us anything about his private life. We didn't know he was seeing anyone regularly. When did you meet?'

Emily wished she'd talked this through in a little more detail with Loukas. What if she said something that contradicted something he'd already said? Had he told them about their engagement or had they found out via the media? He didn't appear all that close to them. His manner towards them was polite but distant, almost to the point of being cold. 'Erm…we met through mutual friends.'

'I'm so thrilled for you both,' Phyllida said. 'I never thought he was ever going to get married. You must be a very special person.'

'She is,' Loukas said, slipping his arm around Emily's waist.

Emily smiled until her face ached. What was it with Loukas and his mother and sister? They didn't exchange hugs or kisses with him like a normal family would do. She wasn't sure what to say or do to ease the stilted atmosphere. She'd thought her relationship with her mother was a little awkward at times, but even a stiff broomstick hug and an air kiss was better than nothing.

'It's wonderful news about the baby,' his mother

said. 'I wasn't sure I was ever going to be a grand-mother. Are you keeping well?'

'I'm having a bit of trouble with nausea but otherwise I'm okay.'

'We won't stay long,' Ariana said to Emily. 'We just wanted to meet you in person.' Her gaze moved to Loukas. 'I know you don't like impromptu guests but we couldn't stay away this time.'

'You are welcome here any time.' Loukas's voice was unusually husky.

Emily couldn't help noticing the way Ariana kept glancing at Emily's abdomen with an almost wistful expression on her face. Was she worried she might never have the opportunity to marry and have children herself? How bad was her disability? Would it be rude to ask?

'I'm really happy for you, Loukas. I mean that,' Ariana said.

His expression gave little away but his voice still contained that deep, gravelly note. 'Thank you.'

'So when's the wedding?' Phyllida asked with an expectant air.

'In two weeks' time,' Loukas said. 'We're not having a big ceremony, so don't feel you have to attend.'

'But of course we'd love to come, wouldn't we, Ariana?' his mother asked.

'I wouldn't miss it for anything,' Ariana said. 'Although, if you'd rather not have us there…?'

'I would love you to be there,' Emily said. 'In fact, would you be my bridesmaid, Ariana? My best friend Allegra will be my maid of honour but I'd love it if you would be my bridesmaid.' The invitation was out before she had time to think about it. Why was she organising a bridesmaid when, strictly speaking, this wasn't a real wedding? Or at least, not the normal kind. Loukas didn't want a big ceremony, but she couldn't imagine having a wedding without a bridesmaid or two. And who better than his half-sister?

'Are you sure?' Ariana asked with a look of such longing it made something in Emily's chest squeeze, like it was being pinched. 'I've never been in a wedding party before. Are you sure I won't ruin all the photos because of my chair? I can stand for short periods with a bit of support but—'

'Of course you won't spoil the photos,' Emily said. 'How long have you been…? I'm sorry. Am I being rude to ask what happened to you?'

Ariana glanced briefly at Loukas, her teeth momentarily snagging her lower lip. 'Hasn't Loukas told you?'

Emily's stomach shifted like a shoe on a slippery surface. 'Told me what?'

Phyllida put her hand on Ariana's shoulder, her gaze troubled. 'Come on, love. It's time you had a rest. Emily too must be exhausted after the flight. We've taken up too much of your time already.'

'No, no, of course you haven't,' Emily said, glancing at Loukas, but his expression was in its customary locked-down position. What hadn't he told her about his sister's disability? Why hadn't he told her he even had a sister? What was going on? Why was the atmosphere between him and his mother and sister so strained and awkward?

Phyllida and Ariana left the room, the whisper of the wheelchair's tyres over the carpet the only sound in the cavernous silence. Emily turned back to Loukas once the door closed quietly behind them. 'I've felt elephants in the room before, but that one was a woolly mammoth.'

'Leave it, Emily. Please.' He made to leave the room but she caught up to him just in time and snagged him by the arm.

'Tell me what I'm supposed to know,' she said, looking up into his tightly set features.

He put his hand over hers to remove it but she dug her fingers in. 'It's no concern of yours,' he said.

Emily raised her brows until they threatened to disappear past her hairline. 'No concern of mine?

How can you say that when in two weeks I'm going to be your wife?'

His mouth was so flat his lips had all but disappeared. But then he let out a long breath that sounded as if it had come from some deep, dark place inside him. 'I was the one who caused the accident.'

Emily couldn't swallow her gasp of shock in time. He had caused the accident that had maimed his sister? She clutched at her throat with one hand, her heart shuddering at the thought of the burden of guilt he must feel. 'Oh, no...'

'I ran into Ariana with my car. I didn't see her in time. She lost control of the new bike she'd got for her birthday and careened down the driveway and on to the road straight in front of me.' His throat rose and fell before he continued. 'I slammed on the brakes but I... I'd only had my licence a few weeks. I didn't have the experience or the skill to avoid her.'

He had been so young himself—a teenager on the threshold of adulthood—only to be assailed with guilt that would last a lifetime. How devastating for him to be responsible for causing such hurt and suffering, even if it had been an accident. 'Oh, Loukas, that's so awful and tragic. I'm so sorry for your sister and for you. It must have been a nightmare.'

Long remembered anguish was etched in the landscape of his face. 'I thought I'd killed her at first. But then she started screaming.' He took another deep breath and released it in a staggered stream. 'She was in an induced coma for a month and spent a year in hospital and another six months in rehab. I've lost count of the number of surgeries she's had. The most recent one was the week before Draco's wedding, in an effort to get her walking again, but so far it's failed.'

'And all this time you've been blaming yourself,' Emily said, seeing it written not just on his face but also in the way he held his body. Was that why he avoided commitment? Why he had avoided marriage and kids of his own—because of the guilt he carried over that terrible day?

The look he gave her was grimly resigned and he removed her hand from his arm. 'Wouldn't you blame yourself?'

She ran her tongue over her carpet-dry lips. Of course she would if she had been in the same situation. Who wouldn't? No decent person wanted to hurt another person and see them suffer and struggle for years and years with the physical damage. The guilt would gnaw away at even the toughest, most resilient personality. 'Yes, but it was an accident. You didn't mean to hit her. Little kids are accident magnets. They run in and out of danger all the time. It could've happened to anyone coming along that road at that moment. And maybe, if someone else had been coming faster than you, then she wouldn't have survived at all.'

His gaze was ghosted with bone-deep sadness. 'If I had been even five seconds earlier or later she wouldn't have been hit at all.'

Emily reached out to comfort him. 'You have to stop blaming yourself, Loukas. It happened and she survived—that's the main thing.'

He eased away as if her touch made him uncomfortable. Or maybe it was because he wasn't used to talking about the accident. Emily was sure Allegra knew nothing about it, which meant Draco probably didn't either. Why hadn't Loukas told his best friend about the most tragic event of his life? Or was his guilt too burdensome to share? His aloofness had struck her from the first moment she'd met him at the wedding. But now she understood why he kept himself separate from other people. An invisible wall of guilt locked him in his own private prison.

'My mother's marriage broke up the year after the accident,' he said after a moment.

Emily frowned. 'But surely you're not blaming yourself for that too?'

'They were fine until the accident. Her husband

Frank couldn't forgive me for what I'd done, and my mother couldn't forgive him for saying it to my face at every opportunity he could.'

'But lots of marriages break up when there's a sick or disabled child involved,' she said. 'It strains the steadiest of relationships. You shouldn't have been blamed for it. Your mother was right in standing up for you. I would've done the same in a heartbeat.'

He dragged a hand down his face as if to wipe away the memory of that time. 'My mother has been through two bitter divorces because of me. Firstly with my father and then with Frank.'

'Is that why you've always avoided marriage?' Emily asked. 'Because you think you'll somehow jinx it?'

'I hurt people without even trying,' he said. 'I've been doing it all my life.'

She put her hand back on his arm, firmer this time, so he couldn't so easily shrug her off. 'You haven't hurt me, Loukas. The pregnancy was an accident. You're doing all you can to support the baby and me. That's not the behaviour of man who intentionally wants to hurt people. That's the behaviour of a man who's mature and stable enough to face even the toughest of responsibilities.'

His expression had gone back to its default setting of inscrutable mask. 'Since you've asked Ariana to be your bridesmaid, I take it you've finally come to terms with our marriage going ahead?'

A part of Emily wished she hadn't been quite so impulsive in offering his sister the role of bridesmaid. It was like passing a point of no return. She hadn't realised he would use it as a way to bend her to his will if she'd had second thoughts. But the streak of ruthlessness in his personality was a reminder of the lengths he would go to achieve a goal. He wanted to be an involved father to their child. He wanted to provide for and protect it, as any decent dad worthy of the title would want to do. But why shouldn't she give him this chance to move on from his tragic past, to help him heal, by sharing the parenting of their accidental baby for as long as they stayed together?

Besides that, she cared about him. The more she learned about him, the more she cared. He was a complex man with hidden depths she wanted to explore. Hadn't she sensed that the first time she'd met him? Why else had she spent that crazily out-of-character night with him? Something about him had spoken to her on a level no one else had ever reached before. 'I know you don't want a big wedding, but I could see how much she'd love to be involved. I really like your mum and your sister. But you seem so stilted with them, even though they don't seem to blame you for the accident.'

He put some distance between their bodies, turning his back to stare at the view of the ocean below. It was as if a wall had come up around him. An invisible, impenetrable wall that had 'Keep Out' written all over it.

'They are nothing but gracious. But I'm aware every time I'm around them I remind them of my part in Ariana's disability. She's in a wheelchair, for God's sake. I put her there. She can't have the life every other young woman her age takes for granted.'

Emily came up behind him and stroked her hand down his stiffly held shoulders to the small of his back. 'It's tragic she's not able to walk but it might not be for ever. There are medical breakthroughs happening all the time. And she does have a life. It might not be the one she would have chosen, but that doesn't mean it's not fulfilling and worthwhile.'

He turned his head to look down at her. 'Look, I know you mean well, but it's not just Ariana's life that's been ruined. My mother is stuck in the role of full-time carer.'

'But maybe that's what she wants,' Emily said.

His eyes contained a bleakness that reminded her of a lonely and deserted moor. 'Maybe, but her life would've been better if she'd had a choice. I took that away from her.' He brushed past her to leave the room, almost colliding with his housekeeper coming through the doorway. 'Excuse me,' he said to Chrystanthe. 'I have some business to see to. Can you settle Emily into my room?'

The master bedroom Chrystanthe led Emily to was decorated in muted greys and stark white with subtle touches of blue. The king-sized bed had a velvet and studded Venetian-style headboard in a deeper shade of mushroom-grey, and there was a collection of plump pillows, both standard and European, and a velvet throw over the foot of the bed. Twin bedside tables balanced the massive bed, and the lamps with their dove-grey shades were a nice counter to the crystal chandelier above. The large windows were festooned with gorgeous white drapes with grey velvet piping featured on the pelmet above.

But, while supposedly it was Loukas's bedroom, at first glance there was little to tie him to it. It didn't have any personal touches such as photos or family memorabilia. While his clothes were arranged neatly in the walk-in wardrobe, and his toiletries in the *en suite* bathroom, the bedroom itself looked more like a luxury hotel suite than anything else. How much time did he spend at his villa? She knew he travelled a lot for work but if this was his base then it sure could do with a few little homey touches. It was almost *too* perfect. She couldn't imagine a sticky-fingered toddler coming in here… Well, she could, but it wasn't a pretty sight.

'Loukas is always working too hard,' Chrystanthe said, smoothing down the already impossibly smooth throw on the end of the bed. 'Maybe you will teach him to relax and enjoy life a bit more, *ne*?'

'I'll try,' Emily said. 'How long have you worked for him?'

'Five years. He is a good boss. Very generous. I want for nothing and neither do any of his staff.'

'Do his mother and sister visit often?'

'This is the first time in nearly four years,' Chrystanthe said, giving the pillows a quick plump. 'He is often travelling, you know? But he more than makes up for it by spoiling them with wonderful gifts. The cruise he sent them on was an exclusive one with their own private butler and chef. He flies them wherever they want to go in a private jet so Ariana doesn't have to suffer any delays or discomfort flying on a commercial airline. Her chair is custom-made. He pays for every medical expense and he lavishes them both with gifts at Christmas and on birthdays.'

Emily suspected Loukas would have been generous even without the guilt that plagued him. He was that sort of man. He didn't use his wealth to build himself up but to help others. But what if his mother and sister wanted less of his gifts and more of him? Could she help him with that? Perhaps build a bridge so he could be more comfortable around them and they with him?

Chrystanthe put the last pillow in place. 'Now, can I get you a cup of tea or a cool drink?'

'No, I'm fine,' Emily said, glancing longingly at the bed. 'I'll just have a lie down for a bit.'

The housekeeper closed the door softly behind her as Emily lay down. She closed her eyes, promising herself she would only have forty winks...

Loukas walked out of the villa to the olive grove he'd planted when he'd first bought the property. His mother and sister showing up like that had rocked him so much he had barely been able to talk. He had never encouraged them to call on him. He occasionally called on them, but he never stayed longer than an hour or two at the most. He provided them with everything they needed and more but, as to spending extended periods of time with them, well, that was asking too much of them, let alone him. He had only invited them to Corfu once, the year after he'd bought the villa, but it had been more out of duty than any desire to play happy families. He'd sent them on a ridiculously expensive cruise of the Greek Isles because he'd thought Ariana needed a distraction after the last bout of surgery that hadn't achieved the result she'd hoped. He knew he should have contacted them before they found out the news online, but any contact with them always made the guilt come back with a cruel vengeance.

He embodied Ariana's lost potential. Every time she saw him she was reminded of what he had done. How could she not be reminded? He was reminded every time he looked at her sitting in that chair. It didn't matter that it had been an accident. His actions had caused irreparable harm and he couldn't undo it. Not one little bit of it. He had seen the wistfulness in his sister's eyes when she'd glanced at Emily's abdomen. Ariana might never have children. The doctors had already warned her the internal damage had all but removed the possibility of having a family. How difficult must it be for her to see him marry Emily and have the family he knew she longed for, as most young women her age did?

Emily had generously invited Ariana to be a bridesmaid and he'd jumped on her gesture to secure even more firmly her agreement to marry him. It was a nice gesture on her part, but it would only intensify his guilt. Would his sister ever get to be a bride? And she couldn't shuffle more than a couple of steps without support. How then would she walk down the aisle of a church? As far as he knew, she hadn't even been on a date. Ariana lived a life of medical appointments and gruelling exercise programs to maintain what little mobility she had left.

Loukas snapped off an olive leaf and tore it into shreds, tossing them to the ground in a parody of tossing confetti. Even the late-afternoon sun seemed to be glaring at him accusingly. He had brought Emily here hoping it would keep her out of the way of the press and instead it had put her smack-bang in the middle of the train wreck of his family.

No matter what he did, he seemed to make things worse.

Emily hadn't realised she'd been asleep until she heard the faint clicking sound of the bedroom door opening. The tall figure of Loukas was framed in the doorway. He softly closed the door and came over to the bed. 'I'm sorry, did I wake you?'

She sat up and pushed the tangle of her hair away from her face. 'I was just dozing. I get so tired, it's unbelievable. How do women have more than a couple of kids? It must be exhausting.'

He sat on the edge of the bed next to her legs. 'Can I get you anything? A drink? Something to eat? Dinner won't be for a while but I can get Chrystanthe to rustle up something if you'd—'

'No, please don't fuss. I'll wait for dinner. I'm looking forward to chatting some more to your mum and Ariana.'

'They won't be joining us, I'm afraid.'

Emily frowned. 'Oh? Why not? Is Ariana not well?'

His eyes shifted from hers. 'They were keen to get back to their cruise. They only got off for a couple of hours so they could meet you.'

'That's a shame. Maybe I could visit them at home to discuss the bridesmaid dress. Where do they live?'

'In Oxfordshire in England.'

'Not in Greece?'

Loukas's expression had a hint of ruefulness. 'After the divorce from my father, my mother went off all things Greek. I bought her and Ariana a house in a village close to the hospital and physical therapy centre Ariana goes to. The house has an indoor therapy pool and a gym so she can continue her exercises at home.'

'You sound like a very generous person,' Emily said. 'Chrystanthe was telling me what a great boss you are and how good you are to Ariana and your mum.'

His lips gave a humourless on-off movement. 'Let's hope I can be a good husband and father too.'

She placed her hand on his hair-roughened wrist. 'You will be. I'm sure of it.'

His brown eyes meshed with hers, his hand coming over her hand and holding it against his warm, hard thigh. Sensual energy pulsed and throbbed with every beat of Emily's heart. It was as if her blood was speaking to his blood through the skin-to-skin contact of his hand pressing hers to his thigh. She moistened her lips, her gaze slipping to his mouth, watching in breathless anticipation for him to close the distance.

He brought his head down, his lips nudging hers in playful little touches that made her mouth tingle. 'I should let you rest some more.' His deep, husky voice acted like another caress on her fevered senses.

'But I'm not tired now.' She bumped his lips with hers, using her tongue to glide over his lower lip.

Loukas made a groaning sound and gathered her closer, crushing her to him and bringing his mouth down on hers in a drugging kiss that made her insides quake with want. His tongue came in search of hers, teasing it into a sexy samba that mimicked the passionate love-making they had done a month ago. His hands cupped her face, his fingers splaying over her hair as he feasted on her mouth, like a starving man does a long anticipated meal.

Emily returned his kiss with just as much fervour, her senses reeling with each heart-stopping flicker and glide of his tongue. She set to work on his shirt, desperate to get her hands on his bare skin, but with her finger still heavily bandaged she didn't get very far. Loukas took over the task for her and hauled his shirt over his head and tossed it to the floor. He then began on her clothes, undoing buttons, sliding her top off her shoulders, kissing her as he went, drawing out the process until she was squirming with impatience. He left her bra in place and kissed the upper curves of her breasts with gentle barely touching presses of his lips. His concern about her tenderness touched her deeply.

He laid her back against the pillows and kissed his way down from her mouth to her décolletage, his hands cradling her as if she were priceless porcelain. It was different from their first encounter when clothes had been all but ripped off and bodies hard pressed together in an almost animalistic coupling. This was a slow but sure celebration of her body, a worshipful discovery of every curve and contour with his gentle hands, lips and tongue. Every nerve in her body vibrated with the pleasure of his touch, the sensations rippling through her in escalating waves.

It was the most thrilling experience of her life to be touched with such exquisite care. He helped her out of the rest of her clothes, every hair on her head tingling at the roots when he came to the final barrier of her knickers. Not white cotton this time, but dark blue lace, as she'd changed before she'd left to visit Allegra. He traced the seam of her body through the lace of her knickers, the touch so sensual it made her back arch off the bed.

He gently eased her knickers away, her senses so heightened the glide of the fabric against her skin made her sigh in pleasure. Loukas brought his mouth down to her feminine mound, stroking the outside of her form with his tongue just as he had with his finger against the lace. Every cell in her body throbbed with longing, her flesh swelling and delicately scenting with the musk of arousal. He separated her with his fingers, caressed her with his tongue in soft strokes that were slow and measured, before gradually upping the pace in response to her whimpered signals. The ripples started deep and low in her body and then spread

out like a tide, coursing through her body in con-
vulsive waves. Goose bumps rose on her flesh and
hot, fizzing tingles shot up and down her spine
until finally the sensations faded, leaving her in
a blissful afterglow that made all her muscles feel
like melted wax.

Emily opened her eyes to see his glittering with
his own anticipation. She ran a hand down his sternum, past his wash-board abdomen, to her prize
below. His features gave a spasm of pleasure when
she took him in her hand, stroking and caressing
him the way she knew he loved best. 'I guess we
won't be needing a condom,' she said.

Dark heat flared in his eyes. 'I want you.'

'So I can tell.' She gave him another stroke, running her fingertip over the head of his erection.

He pressed her back down, taking care not to let
her take his weight, their legs finding their preferred
positions as if they had been making love together
for years. That was what had struck her about that
night after the wedding. There hadn't been any awk-
wardness between them. Her body had expressed
her desire, as had his, and together they had created
an explosive choreography of intimacy.

He kissed Emily thoroughly, his tongue duelling with hers in another slow tango that ramped
up her desire all over again. She caressed Loukas's

back and shoulders, delighting in the play of his taut muscles as they responded to her touch. She went lower to cup his buttocks, encouraging him to take his pleasure, opening her legs even further, her body on fire for the deep, silken thrust of his.

He made another guttural sound, as if his self-control was teetering at the limit, and then he entered her with a long, smooth surge that made her gasp out loud in relief. The feel of him moving inside her rocked her senses. He was gentle and yet thrillingly male, taking her on a tantalising journey of sensory delight that made every inch of her flesh go into raptures. Her intimate muscles gripped him with each thrust and retreat, the sexy rhythm in perfect tune with her body. He slipped a hand between their bodies, knowing exactly how to intensify her pleasure to give her the extra strokes of friction that would send her over the edge. The orgasm exploded like a massive firework, sending rivers of sensations through her body until she was shaking with the impact.

His low grunt of pleasure followed close behind, the dual rocking of their bodies in that penultimate moment sending another wave of delight crashing through her flesh.

Loukas slowly withdrew, but not before brushing her hair away from her face. 'Are your breasts okay? I didn't crush them too hard with my weight?'

Emily touched his face with her fingertips. 'I forgot all about them, to be honest.'

A smile ghosted his mouth. 'So, I guess that clears that up, then.'

'What? My breasts?'

He coiled a tendril of her hair around his finger. 'It was just as good between us as I imagined. Better, even.'

Emily sent her fingertip around his mouth. 'You were amazingly gentle with me.'

'I've never made love to a pregnant woman before. It's a bit nerve-racking, actually.'

'You don't have to treat me like I'm made of glass.'

He stroked his finger down between her breasts. 'Does this hurt?'

'No.'

He moved his finger to her right breast and traced a lazy circle around her nipple. 'This?'

'No...'

He brought his mouth to her breast, using his tongue to follow the earlier pathway of his finger. The feel of his warm tongue on her sensitive flesh made her skin shiver. 'You have beautiful breasts.'

'Glad you think so,' Emily said. 'I was about

to send out a search party when I was a teenager but thankfully they showed up before my fifteenth birthday.'

This time his slanted smile made his eyes sparkle. 'You have nothing to be worried about, Emily. You are one of the most naturally beautiful women I've ever met.'

She couldn't help basking in the glow of his compliments. Who wouldn't feel beautiful, the way he looked at her? She wasn't a vain person—how could she be with an overbite and freckles and bad eyesight? But every time Loukas looked at her she felt as if she was the most stunning creature in the world. 'I'm not holding out for a *Vogue* shoot any time soon, but thanks anyway.'

He picked up a tendril of her hair again and wound it around his finger, his eyes holding hers in a smouldering lock that made her insides clench all over again with need. 'I want to make love to you again but I don't want to tire you.'

Emily pinched his chin between her finger and thumb and brought his face down to hers. 'Did I say I was tired?'

His lips moulded themselves to hers in a leisurely kiss that had a blistering undercurrent of lust. She opened for him, making a sound of sheer pleasure when his tongue circled hers. His afternoon stubble grazed her face when he changed position, but it only heightened her awareness and need of him. He turned her so she was lying over him, giving her more control and less of his weight to worry about. He placed his hands just below her breasts, offering them gentle support.

Emily swept her hair back over one shoulder, straddling him with her thighs, her body flaring with incendiary heat as his erection rose in front of her mound. She moved against him, letting him feel how ready she was for him.

He sucked in a harsh-sounding breath and groaned. 'You're killing me.'

She leaned over him, planting her hands either side of his head, letting her hair fall forward and tickle his chest. 'Kill me right back.'

Loukas's hands gripped her by the hips and he pushed up into her with another deep groan of satisfaction. The movement of his body in hers incited her to be more daring and adventurous. She moved her body in a circular motion, delighting in the way the friction changed with each movement. Each time his body surged and withdrew, waves of pleasure built in tantalising ripples and coursed through her flesh. She was so close to flying, but couldn't quite lift off, until he came to her rescue by massaging the swollen heart of her, sending her soaring into the abyss on an orgasm so intense she could barely register anything but the sensations ricocheting through her body.

His took his pleasure with a series of thrusts, each one sending a vicarious wave of delight through her intimate flesh. His whole body relaxed back against the mattress, and he brought her down to rest her head against his chest, one of his hands moving in a slow stroke up and down the curve of her spine.

Never had Emily felt so physically close to another person. Love-making with Daniel—when it had infrequently occurred—had often been quick and unsatisfying, for which she had mostly blamed herself. And, because Daniel had gone to any lengths to hide his secret from his overly conservative parents, he too would often allow her to feel it was her fault. For seven years she had felt hopelessly inadequate.

But ever since sleeping with Loukas she'd realised she was more than capable of experiencing earth-shattering orgasms—of being a sexually competent partner who could give and receive pleasure. The chemistry she shared with Loukas wasn't just in bed but in every aspect of her contact with him. She was attracted to his intellect, his quiet strength of character and his dry sense of humour. His sense of responsibility impressed her, the fact that he was prepared to do whatever he could to provide for his child, even though it pushed him out of his comfort zone.

Loukas's hand settled on the small of her back, creating a warm, soothing glow that threatened to melt her bones. Emily lifted her head and, leaning on his chest, toyed with the line of his lower lip with her fingertip. 'I think my mother might be on to something.'

One of his brows lifted. 'Oh? What's that?'

She traced the shallow dip below his lip. 'She teaches couples how to communicate better through having great sex.'

His hand began another slow stroke of her spine, his dark eyes glinting. 'Sounds like the homework could be fun.'

Emily sent her finger over his top lip, playing special attention to the firm philtral ridge running beneath his nose to his mouth. 'Not that it ever worked with my ex.'

'So what happened between you and him?'

You're talking about your ex while you're in bed with Loukas?

I have to tell him some time, don't I? Anyway, it's called communication.

It's called being a gauche idiot, that's what it's called.

Emily focussed on Loukas's stubble-coated Adam's apple rather than meet his gaze. 'In the seven years I dated and lived with Daniel, he forgot to mention he was gay.'

Loukas frowned. 'You didn't suspect anything?'

Emily sighed. 'On reflection, there were lots of indications, but I disregarded them. He comes from a really conservative background. He didn't feel he could ever come out to his parents in case they disowned him, so he hid it since he was a teenager. I think that's why I never suspected anything at the beginning, because he was romantic and attentive and made me feel special. It was only after we started living together that things went downhill. For all of that time I blamed our patchy sex life on myself. We seemed to only ever have sex when he'd had a few drinks. It made me feel he wasn't attracted to me unless he had wine- or beer-goggles on. It wasn't great for my self-esteem, that's for sure.'

'You didn't think about leaving him sooner?'

She gave a self-deprecating grimace. 'I can be pretty stubborn when I know I'm in the wrong. I dig myself in deeper and deeper because I don't want to admit I've made a mistake. Don't get me wrong—

we were good friends…really good friends, but the chemistry wasn't right. Once five years had passed, I got even more desperate to pretend everything was fine. Looking back now, I can see how I'd convinced myself everything was okay with the relationship when in fact it was anything but. The more time that passed, the more determined I was to ignore the signs. All of them were there but I point-blank refused to acknowledge them. I would've made a great attendant on the *Titanic*. I would've had those deck chairs repainted and handed around drinks and conducted the brass band to boot.'

'So how did you find the courage to leave?'

'Here's what I'm really ashamed about,' Emily said. 'I didn't find the courage. Not really. It was only when I found Daniel in bed with his lover when I came home unexpectedly from work one day, I realised I had to finally face up to what was right in front of me. He begged me to stay in the relationship to keep his cover for his parents. He even said we could have kids and the dog I've always wanted as long as I kept his secret. I was angry at first but then I felt so sorry for him. I knew his parents well and I knew exactly what would happen if he came out to them.'

Loukas's forehead was still deeply furrowed.

'You surely weren't going to stay with him after that?'

She pulled at her lip with her teeth. 'I thought about it for a day or two. It was so hard, because I actually loved him, and I truly believe he loved me in his way. But I ended things and moved out and within a few weeks he finally told his parents.'

'How did they take it?'

Emily let out another sigh. 'They haven't quite disowned him but they refuse to accept he's gay. They think it's a stage he's going through or something. They even blamed me for turning him to "the other side". I got the most horrible phone call from his mother accusing me of being such a rubbish partner he had no choice but to look elsewhere for comfort. They refuse to meet his partner, Tim, and they'll only see Daniel if he comes to the house alone. It's terribly sad.'

He touched her face again, his expression suddenly wistful. 'You're a good person, Emily.'

'So are you,' Emily said, holding his gaze.

A shadow moved through Loukas's eyes before he gently moved her aside to vacate the bed. He picked up his trousers and, stepping back into them, zipped them with a sound that sounded suspiciously to Emily like a punctuation mark.

'Let me guess,' she said, sitting upright. 'You have some urgent work to see to?'

A frown flickered over his forehead. 'Emily...' His voice had that note of reproof in it that made her feel like a child who had overstepped the mark. 'You don't understand...'

'I understand more than you give me credit for,' she said. 'I know how guilty you must feel. I can't imagine how painful it must be to—'

'Do you?' he asked, eyes glittering. 'Do you really know what it's like to ruin someone's life and never be able to do anything to fix it?'

Emily swallowed a tight lump as big as a pineapple. 'You can't fix it, but you're not going to help your sister or your mother by keeping your distance. They love you, Loukas. They want to be connected to you, but you seem to prefer to keep them at arm's length. They shouldn't have left this afternoon. They shouldn't have felt they had to go. They shouldn't have had to ask if you wanted them at your wedding. You should've insisted they stay for the rest of the weekend at the very least.'

He dragged a hand down the length of his face, the sound of his palm against his stubble overly loud in the silence. 'When I got back to the villa from a walk they'd already left. Chrystanthe informed me the butler from the cruise had collected them moments earlier.'

'But would you have asked them to stay?'

He let out a long stream of air. 'No, probably not.'

Emily got off the bed and, without bothering to cover herself, came up close to wrap her arms around his waist. She craned her neck to look up at him. 'Perhaps we can ask them to stay a few days before the wedding so I can get to know them better, plus get Ariana's dress sorted. Would you mind?'

His arms came around her to hold her closer. 'It's impossible to deny you anything when you stand naked in front of me. But then, I guess you know that, don't you?'

Emily gave him an impish smile and lifted her mouth to his descending one. 'I was counting on it.'

CHAPTER SEVEN

WHEN EMILY CAME DOWNSTAIRS the following morning, Loukas had already been up for several hours. He had left her to lie in bed, giving her tea and toast and making her promise to rest as long as she wanted. She found him in his study, working at his computer, but he pushed his chair back when she walked in and came over to take both her hands in a gentle hold. 'How are you feeling?'

'Pretty good, actually,' she said. 'I think having that tea and toast first thing really helped.'

He gave her hands a tiny squeeze, his expression guarded. 'Emily, I've made an appointment with my lawyer to see to a pre-nuptial agreement. He'll be here in an hour.'

Emily rolled her lips together, her gaze slipping out of reach of his. A pre-nuptial reminded her of how everything was different about their relationship. She knew it was an insurance policy, and it made sound financial sense for him to insist on one, as it would for any person in a couple who had independent wealth or assets they wanted to protect. But it was an unnerving reminder of the step she was taking—a step that was a long way from her dream of happy-ever-after. 'Fine. That's good. Makes sense to get things on the level from the get-go.'

He lifted her chin with the tip of his finger. 'I know how that must make you feel, but I will be very generous in the event of a divorce.'

'Don't you mean *when* we divorce?'

His mouth tightened for a brief moment and his hand fell back by his side. 'It would be wrong of me to expect you to stay with me indefinitely. It's not what either of us want.'

But what if I do want it?

Uh-oh. I knew this was going to happen.

What?

You're falling in love with him.

Emily pushed away the thought as if she were shoving something to the back of her wardrobe. She would sort it out later. Much later. Of course she wasn't in love with him. How could she be? Just because they had smoking-hot sex didn't mean they were Mr and Mrs Happy Ever After. It meant they had awesome chemistry—that was all. 'Right, of course,' she said. 'But it just sounds a little weird to be going into marriage with the idea of a divorce being a given rather than a possibility.'

'There is no need for our divorce to be anything but civil and entirely mutual.'

He made it sound so polite and clinical. How far away from her dream of a fairy-tale relationship was this heading? But she had to remember the baby. She was only agreeing to this because of the child they had made together. She owed it to their baby at least to give Loukas a chance to be a present and actively engaged father. She had seen too many fathers distanced from their children in messy break-ups. Even the most devoted fathers were often thwarted by custodial arrangements in the event of a separation or divorce. This way she could give Loukas a chance to build a solid relationship with their child, but she wouldn't be tying either herself or Loukas down indefinitely.

His phone rang in his pocket and he fished it out, mouthed, 'Excuse me,' and answered it. He spoke in fluent Greek and she listened with one ear while her gaze drifted to his immaculately tidy desk. Unlike hers, which always looked like a child with a temper tantrum had taken to it. She was close enough to see what was open on his computer screen. Her heart gave a funny little skip. It was a popular and informative pregnancy site she had looked at herself. It touched her that he was showing an interest in the development of their baby. It was easy for fathers to feel shunted aside by the process of pregnancy and childbirth but he obviously wanted to equip himself with as much knowledge as he could.

Loukas put away his phone. 'Sorry about that. I was waiting on an important call.'

Emily pointed to the screen. 'Have you found that site helpful?'

His expression was too inscrutable to be described as sheepish but she couldn't help feeling he'd been caught a little off-guard. 'Yes and no.'

Emily frowned. She had found it the most helpful of all the sites she'd checked. 'Why no?'

He looked as though he was trying to swallow something too big for his oesophagus. 'Things can go wrong during pregnancy.'

'Like miscarriage?'

His eyes flinched, as if blinking away a horrible thought. 'Women still die in childbirth. It might be not as common as a hundred years ago but it does still happen.'

Emily wondered what had triggered him looking at the website. Was it concern for *her*, rather than interest in the baby's development? 'Why did you look at the website?'

His face got that boxed-up look about it she had come to know so well. 'It has been a long time since I sat in a Sex Ed class.'

She fought back a smile. 'Me too. I don't think I heard anything about morning sickness and extreme fatigue. I just remember condoms and courgettes and squirming with embarrassment at the snickering boys.'

A smile tilted his mouth, transforming his features and bringing life to his eyes. But then a shadow passed over Loukas's face, dimming his gaze. 'Are you worried about what could happen to you?'

'Well, I guess I'm not so keen on getting stretch marks.'

He was still frowning in that I'm-being-serious-and-this-is-no-time-for-jokes manner. 'I read about a condition where the amniotic fluid leaks into the mother's bloodstream and it's virtually always fatal. Then there's post-partum haemorrhage. A mother can bleed out in minutes if help isn't available.'

'I'm not going to die, Loukas,' Emily said, in a joint effort to reassure herself as well as him. She had skated over the risks section on the site. Her image of childbirth was a pink-faced, bunny-rug-wrapped infant in an exhausted but blissful mother's arms with a doting husband and father present. Nowhere in her imaginings had there been any emergency blood transfusions, crash trolleys and panic-stricken doctors.

Loukas didn't look all that convinced. 'And the risks actually escalate if it's a twin birth.'

Emily laughed. 'Will you stop it? It's bad enough accidentally falling pregnant with one baby, let alone two.'

A beat of silence passed.

'Give me your hand,' she said.

Loukas held it out and Emily placed it on her tummy, which was a little podgy for someone who was only a month into a pregnancy. But, given she was a comfort eater from way back, that was not so surprising. A family block of fruit and nut choco-late had to go somewhere and her tummy seemed to be where it had chosen. 'In a couple of months you'll be able to feel knees and elbows wriggling around in there.'

A look of awe passed over his face. 'Can you feel anything yet?'

'No, it's way too early,' she said. 'It's weird to think a new life is in there getting its act together, isn't it?'

He removed his hand after a long moment. 'We should discuss names at some point. And if we want to know the sex of the baby before it's born. Would you like to know?'

'Would you?'

'You can make the decision, Emily. You're the one doing all the hard work, so surely you deserve that privilege.'

She gave him a rueful look. 'I used to think I'd want to be surprised when it's born, but I figure you're a little over surprises, right?'

One corner of his mouth twitched. 'You can say that again.'

The lawyer arrived a short time later and the business of the pre-nuptial agreement was over soon after. As if to soften the blow, Loukas took Emily for a short walk through an olive grove to have a picnic in a secluded cove not far from his villa. The fringe of cypress pines provided some much-needed shade from the intensely hot sun, and she sat on the rug he'd laid down on the sand and looked longingly at the view of the sparkling ocean just metres away.

'I wish I'd brought bathers,' Emily said when he came down beside her on the rug. 'I was in such a mad dash to pack the other night, I didn't think to put some in.'

'You won't need them here,' Loukas said. 'I own this cove and it's completely hidden from the top

of the cliff. The nearest road is at least three kilo-
metres away.'

She turned to peer over her shoulder at the cliff
path they'd come down, as if expecting to see a
cluster of paparazzi with long-range lenses. 'Are
you sure?'

He slid a warm hand down from the middle of
her shoulder blades to the dip in her spine, making
every muscle in her body sigh with pleasure. 'I've
swum down here heaps of times.'

'Naked?'

'Yes.'

'Alone or with someone?'

He picked up a small twig off the rug and tossed
it onto the sand near his crossed ankles. 'Alone. I
haven't brought anyone down here with me before
you.'

Emily glanced at him but he was staring at the
twig he'd tossed with a part-frown on his face. 'Why
did you bring me?'

He turned his head to look at her, his expression
difficult to read. 'How about that swim? Do you
want to have lunch or cool off first?'

Emily chewed at her lip. 'I've never swum naked
before. What if something bites me? And I have to
take my contacts out, unless you happen to have a
pair of swimming goggles handy.'

He rummaged in the bag where he'd packed towels and sunscreen and handed her a pair of blue goggles. *'Voilà.'*

Loukas walked hand in hand with Emily to the water, making sure she didn't lose her footing on the hot sand. She kept grinning up at him like a kid who had been given permission to do something that was decidedly wicked. 'Are you absolutely sure no one can see me? Scout's honour?'

He gave her hand a gentle squeeze. 'You're perfectly safe with me.' As soon as he said the words, his gut clenched. Was she safe? He had made sure she stayed in bed and rested that morning because he'd read on that website how pregnancy nausea hit hard first thing on an empty stomach. That wretched website was giving him nightmares. So much could go wrong when a woman was pregnant. He had gone online out of curiosity about the process of pregnancy…or so he'd told himself. It was only after he realised how obsessed he was becoming that he understood it had more to do with Emily than with the baby. The baby was important to him in a distant sense, but Emily was present, and had such a potent effect on his senses. Not just his senses. That was the scary part. He was developing a thing about her.

What the hell was a thing?

He had never felt this way before. He kept putting it down to the fact she was pregnant but he couldn't help feeling it was more than that. He genuinely liked her. She made him smile. Who had ever done that to him before? She was fresh and honest and didn't live on the surface of life, like some of the women he'd dated. She dug deeper. A little too deep for his liking, but in a way it had been a relief to tell her about the accident. Telling her hadn't eased his guilt but it had eased his burden. Someone else knew what he felt. Empathised with him.

He had been careful how he'd broached the subject of the pre-nup because he hadn't wanted to upset her. He had never brought anyone down to his cove before because it was his private sanctuary, but it seemed fitting to share it with Emily and their developing child. He'd had some qualms about her walking down the cliff path but she had done it without even drawing breath. The sun was scorching, and her skin was a lot lighter than his, but he'd lathered her with sunscreen and only just stopped himself from making love to her on the rug because she was feeling so hot.

That was another thing he'd read about pregnancy—the mother shouldn't let her core body temperature get too high because it could harm the baby.

The baby.

Every time he thought of those two words he would start to imagine their child. Would it look like him? Would it be a girl or boy? Emily wouldn't show for weeks, if not months, but he couldn't help wondering what it would be like to see their baby on an ultrasound. Would that make it seem more real to see those tiny developing limbs and body? That tiny heartbeat? He wondered what it would be like to see his child born. To hear that first cry. To hold it in his arms for the first time.

What sort of father would he be?

Loukas hadn't expected to feel anything for the baby at this stage and yet, the more he thought about that tiny developing body, the more he got a warm feeling in his chest.

Almost as warm as the feeling he got when he thought of Emily…

Emily smiled up at him once they were waist-deep in the water. 'You can let me go now. I won't fall over.'

'In a minute.' He brought her closer so her body was slick and cool and wet as a seal's against his. 'There's something I want to do first.' He pressed his mouth to hers and she gave a soft whimper of pleasure—the same little whimper that had wreaked such havoc on his control the night of the wedding. Her mouth was like a flower opening, soft and fragrant, and sweet as nectar. Her tongue shyly met his and then became bolder as he deepened the kiss. He held her by the hips, holding against the pounding heat of his body, wanting her so badly it was an ache that dragged at his flesh. She pushed herself even closer, her arms going around his neck, her fingers tugging and releasing his hair as her mouth stayed fused to his.

After a long, blissful moment, he moved his mouth from hers to kiss a pathway down the side of her neck, to the spot below her earlobe that never failed to get a breathless gasp out of her. He used the tip of his tongue around the shell of her ear, tracing the delicate whorls, until she turned her head to press her mouth back to his in a hungry 'I want you' kiss that made the blood roar through his veins like a freight train. She reached for him, her soft little hands massaging and stroking him before she brought him to her entrance, raising herself on tiptoes to give him access.

He needed no other invitation.

Loukas was inside her with a thrust that made every hair on his head tingle, her body clutching at him, rippling around him as tight as a fist. She moved with him, her little moans and gasps spurring him on, ramping up his desire until he was fighting not to lose control before he made sure she was satisfied. He slipped one of his hands beneath the water to find the heart of her, taking her over the edge with a few strokes of his fingers. She came apart around him, her body convulsing with pleasure that triggered his own.

The sun beating down on his back, the cool water lapping at their bodies and Emily's gasping cries of ecstasy brought to the experience an earthy, elemental quality he had never experienced before.

She gave a long, shuddering sigh and met his gaze with a sparkling look. 'Wow. Swimming has never been so much fun before.'

Loukas gave a soft laugh and brushed a droplet of seawater away from her cheek. 'Likewise.'

She planted her hands on his chest, her lower body snug against his, her toffee-brown eyes luminous. 'Do you know, that's the first time I've ever heard you laugh?'

He had never felt like laughing before he met her. She was a fun person to be around with her sunny, optimistic disposition. When he was around her, he felt alive in a way he hadn't in years. He looked forward to being with her. Wasn't that why he'd sought her out in London? He'd wanted to feel that kick in his blood, that spring in his step, and that fire in his belly that he only got when she was near. He looked down at the soft bow of her mouth and gave a crooked smile. 'Maybe there's some hope for me after all.'

CHAPTER EIGHT

EMILY SPENT THE next few days with Loukas, looking at some of the sites on Corfu. At first he wasn't keen on the idea of going to the most popular tourist places, in case they were spotted by members of the press or public, but Emily was keen to see more of the beautiful island he called home. They had lunch each day in quaint little restaurants or cafés and wandered around the ancient streets, archaeological museums, art galleries and churches, such as the spectacular Church of St Sypridion. There was a visit to the magnificent Mount Pantokrator, the highest mountain on the island.

After they came back from the mountain, Emily spied an antique shop in the Old Town. 'Can I have a look in there?'

'Sure.'

She walked in and smelt the passage of time. Lots of time. Whole centuries of it. She browsed through the shop, stopping to pick up pieces that snared her interest. While Loukas was occupied with a phone call, she caught sight of a faded blue velvet jewellery box sitting on a shelf next to a collection of early Greek coins. The box was probably more trash than treasure, but Emily couldn't help thinking of the woman or women who had stored their jewellery in it. It had a lock but no key, and when she opened the lid she felt sure she could smell history. She closed the lid and put it back on the shelf. It wasn't expensive at all but she didn't have her purse with her and she couldn't imagine Loukas buying something so unsophisticated.

'So why did you choose to live on Corfu?' Emily asked over coffee a little while later. 'You're not originally from here, are you?'

Loukas stirred his coffee even though she knew he didn't take sugar. 'No, but I liked it from the first time I came here as a kid on a holiday with my parents before they divorced.'

'Were they ever happy together?'

His mouth turned down at the corners. 'No. My father wasn't ready for marriage—he still isn't, to be frank. But it's a long-held custom in Greece that gaining parental blessing of your marriage partner is essential to a happy union. My father's parents knew my mother and stated their approval.'

'So it was an arranged marriage?'

'Strictly speaking, no. He let my mother think he was in love and then, once he had a wedding ring on her finger and got his parents off his back, he had affair after affair with other women.'

Emily frowned. 'But she loved him?'

He gave her a grim look. 'Not for long. But it took years for her to convince him to give her a divorce. He didn't want his parents to think it was his fault, of course, so he cooked up a whole lot of lies and made her life a miserable hell.'

'And yours too, by the sound of it,' Emily said. 'Do you see much of him these days?'

He pushed his coffee away. 'No. I limit my contact to cards at Christmas and for his birthday.'

'What about Father's Day?'

He gave her a speaking look. 'I never seem to be able to find one that has the most fitting message. "You're a terrible father" isn't usually available.'

Emily couldn't help a giggle escaping. 'And here I was thinking my mother was bad. She's not, by the way. Annoying at times, but definitely not bad.' She frowned and went on. 'I hope she doesn't embarrass you at the wedding. You don't mind if she comes, do you? I know you said it's a quiet ceremony, and to be perfectly honest there is nothing about my mother that's quiet, but I'd like her to be there.'

His mouth slanted in one of his rare smiles. 'Of course she must come.'

Emily played with her teaspoon for a moment. 'Thing is…my mum is a bit of a detective when it comes to relationships. She reckons she can tell at twenty paces if a couple are well suited or not. Apparently, it's all in their body language or something.'

His long, tanned fingers reached for hers, sending a warm tide of longing straight to her core when he stroked the fleshy part of her palm in slow, tantalising circles. 'It kind of makes sense when you think about it.'

She looked at his hand and a frisson went through her at the thought of what magic those fingers could make her feel. 'I told her we're in love. I had to, otherwise she would've gone ballistic about throwing my life away on another dead-end relationship.'

His fingers stalled their movement for a brief second. 'Are you worried about lying to her?'

'Yes. No. Maybe.'

I'm more worried about lying to myself.

He gave her hand a light pat and then sat back in his chair, signalling to the waitress for the bill. 'Come on. It's time we got you out of this sun before you melt.'

I melted a month ago, when you first kissed me.

* * *

Emily was waking from a rest a couple of days later when Loukas came in with a silver-wrapped rectangular package tied with a black ribbon in his hand. He sat on the edge of the bed next to her and handed it to her. 'Remember that antique shop we visited the other day?' he asked. 'I went back to get this for you.'

She took the package and unwrapped it to find the faded antique jewellery box she had admired. She hadn't realised Loukas had even seen her looking at it, as he'd been on the phone to one of his clients while she'd been browsing the shop. It touched her he'd not only noticed but gone back to purchase it for her. Not that it was expensive. It was probably worth less than the price tag stated, but the fact he'd noticed she'd been taken with it moved her deeply. 'Oh, how sweet of you,' she said, stroking the velvet.

'Open it.'

Emily lifted the lid to find two sets of earrings inside: a set of creamy pearl droplets and two winking diamond studs. She didn't need to see any price tags to know they were hideously expensive. 'Oh, they're so beautiful!' She picked up the droplet earrings and draped them over her fingers. Then she picked up the diamond studs and turned them to allow the light to catch their brilliance. She glanced at Loukas, suddenly feeling shy. 'You're too generous. They look terribly expensive.'

'You said you kept losing your jewellery, so I figured the box will help you keep it safe,' he said. 'It has a lock and a tiny key. See?' He pointed to the miniature lock on the base of the box. 'The original key was missing but I've had another one made up.' He fished in his shirt pocket and, taking out a miniscule key, placed it in the centre of her palm and closed her fingers over it to keep it secure.

Emily met his gaze, wondering if he would ever hand her the key to his heart for safekeeping. 'I don't know what to say, other than thank you. No one has ever given me such gorgeous things before.'

'Then it's time someone did.' He brought her hand up to his mouth and pressed a soft kiss to it, holding her eyes with the dark intensity of his.

Emily placed the key next to the jewellery box and then tiptoed her fingers along his lean jaw. 'I've never met anyone like you before.'

Argh! Don't do this!

I have to. I can't deny it any longer. I love him.

Don't say I didn't warn you.

Something flickered through his eyes, like a lightning flash of regret. Then he gave a slow blink, as if preparing to deliver an unpleasant lecture. 'Emily...'

She put a finger over his mouth as if she were pressing a pause button. 'No. Please don't say it. I can't help feeling the way I feel. I love you.'

Loukas let out a long sigh and took her hand away from his face. 'Look, the gifts are just gifts, okay? They don't mean anything.'

Emily refused to believe it. The jewellery box might be worth nothing but the earrings, as well as the engagement ring, were worth more than she earned in a year. *Two* years. How could he say they didn't mean anything? 'Do you buy everyone you sleep with gifts?'

He got up from the bed to stand a few feet away, his eyes so masked they were like the boarded-up windows of a deserted building. 'Yes.'

Her heart shrank away from her chest wall as if it had been punched. 'So...you're saying I'm nothing special?'

He closed his eyes and leaned his head right back, as if searching the heavens for guidance. Then he let out a long breath and returned his gaze to hers. 'No. I'm not saying that. You're incredibly special.'

'But you don't love me.'

He came back to the bed and sat beside her again.

He took her nearest hand and held it in his. Her cut finger had recently healed but now a new wound was opening up inside her heart and it was a thousand times more painful. 'I'm not sure I'm capable of feeling that way about anyone.' He gave her hand a gentle press, the set of his mouth rueful. 'I know it's a cliché, but it's not you, it's me.'

Emily looked down at their joined hands. Why had she blurted out her feelings like that? What had it achieved? A big, fat nothing. She'd made a fool of herself yet again. When would she ever learn?

Told you so.

What was she doing, settling for a relationship that was less than perfect? How could she marry him, in the vain hope he might change at some point in the future? He was only marrying her out of duty, not because he loved her. He desired her, but how long would that last? How long before he called time on their marriage? She would have to live with the threat of it ending instead of the joy of building up a long and lasting relationship together. That wasn't what she'd planned for her life. She wanted to be loved for who she was, treasured and adored the way she had dreamed of for so long. Having a family was supposed to be born out of enduring love. How could she bring a child into a relationship that wasn't based on mutual love?

Emily pulled out of his hold and got off the bed.
'I'm sorry, Loukas, but I can't go on with this a
moment longer.'

A frown made a map of lines across his forehead.
'What are you talking about?'

She met his gaze head-on. 'This marriage you're
proposing. I'm not comfortable with it. Not any of
it. I don't care if it's a small ceremony or a big one.
I don't care if no one is there, or every relative and
person we know and half of Greece is there. The
one thing that should be there and won't be is your
love for me.'

He made to reach out to her but she held up her
hand like a stop sign. 'No. Don't try and talk me
out of it. You're the one who talked me into this
ridiculous plan in the first place. I should never
have agreed to it. I'm going back to London. Our
engagement is over.'

A muscle clenched at the side of his mouth as if
he was trying to control an involuntary tic. 'This is
crazy. You're not thinking straight—'

'That's exactly what I *am* doing,' Emily said.
'I'm thinking how wrong it is to bring a child into
a relationship that has a clock ticking on it. Who
does that? It's not what I want for my life. I want the
fairy-tale; I'm not ashamed of wanting it, either. It's
what most people want—to be loved. I stayed in a

loveless relationship for seven years. Every one of those years I lived in hope, wishing things would get better, but they never did. I can't afford to give up any more of my life to a relationship that isn't working for me.'

'I told you from the start what I was prepared to give you,' he said. 'I haven't made promises or pretended things I don't feel. I want to be involved in my child's life. I don't want my child to be punished because of my mistake.'

That was how he saw his relationship with her—as a mistake. Loukas had offered her a one-night fling and it had come with consequences. Consequences he had been prepared to take responsibility for but with conditions she couldn't accept. Not now she loved him. She knew he felt wretchedly guilty about the accident, but it didn't mean he had to punish himself for the rest of his life, denying himself normal human feelings in a quest to right the wrongs of the past. Who had control over love anyway? It happened no matter what you did to avoid it. She hadn't expected to fall in love with him, it had crept up on her. Each kiss, each touch, each time he made love to her, the feelings had blossomed and grown until she could no longer ignore them.

Emily shook her head at him. 'That's the kicker

right there. You see me as a mistake. That's how you see our baby. An accident you're now dutifully dealing with, just like you dutifully deal with your mother and sister. I don't want to be dealt with dutifully, Loukas, I want to be dealt with devotedly. I deserve it and so do you.'

His expression was as stony as one of the ancient walls of the Old Town they had walked past a few days ago. 'You say you love me, so why are you leaving?'

'Because in the long run it will hurt you if I stay,' Emily said. 'It will hurt me and it will hurt our baby too. I won't stop you being involved. You can come to the twelve-week scan, if you like, and of course the birth, if you want to.'

His hands were shoved in his trouser pockets as if he was determined not to touch her, although she sensed there was a struggle going on inside him, for a tiny muscle in his jaw was working overtime. 'What about the press? They'll hound you for a statement.'

Emily started packing her things but her hands wouldn't seem to co-operate. She couldn't fold a thing but had to scrunch her clothes into creased balls. She would not cry. She would not cry. She *must* not cry. The tears welled in her eyes but she stoically blinked them away. Her chest ached as though someone had wrenched apart her ribcage and torn out her heart but she continued to snatch her belongings from wherever she had last left them: her watch from the bedside table. Her phone charger from the power point next to the bed. Her make-up bag from the bathroom. She worked like an automaton—a robot programmed to complete a task. But inside she wanted to throw herself to the ground like a hysterical child and pummel the floor with her hands and heels.

Why don't you love me? Why? Why? Why?

'I would never say anything bad about you,' she said at last. 'I'll simply tell them the truth. I've changed my mind about marrying you, but we will be co-parenting our child, and look forward to its birth, like any other parents.'

'Leave that,' he said, jerking his head towards the things she'd thrown in a jumble on the bed. 'I'll get Chrystanthe to pack them for you.'

She looked at the pile of clothes and the jewellery he'd given her and swallowed a thick knot in her throat. 'I can leave the jewellery and the box. You might like to give it to someone—'

'Take it,' he said, turning away as if it no longer concerned him what she did.

In the end she took the box but not the jewellery. She left the ring and earrings on the bedside table, locked the box with the little key to keep the lid secure and slipped it into her handbag while he had his back turned to her.

'I need to get a flight,' Emily said, brushing her hair back with her hand, suddenly a little over-whelmed at what she was doing. This was the problem with not being single for so long. You didn't know how to do stuff any more. When was the last time she had booked a flight for herself? Daniel had always done the flights when they'd gone anywhere. It had been his job, just as it had been his job to take out the garbage and empty the dishwasher. Even the flight to Allegra's wedding had been booked for her by Draco. She fought down the panic.

Breathe. Breathe. Breathe. You can do this.

She glanced at Loukas and saw he already had his phone out. What did that mean? That he was keen to see her go?

'I'll book you a flight,' he said in a curt, business-like voice, which she took as a sign she was doing the right thing by leaving. If he loved her he would have been on his knees begging her to stay. He would have been smothering her with kisses and caresses, telling her he couldn't live without her. He certainly wouldn't be whipping out his phone to book her on the next available flight.

She kept her expression composed but inside she was screaming, *Don't let me leave!*

Emily didn't get the chance to say goodbye to Chrystanthe because it was the housekeeper's night off. She scribbled a short note, thanking her for everything, and left it propped on the kitchen counter while Loukas carried her bag out to the car.

The drive to the airport was painfully silent.

Even to the point where Loukas helped her check in to the private jet he'd organised, she hoped he would say something. Anything. But it was as if he was seeing to the departure of an acquaintance. He didn't touch her. He barely even looked at her and, when he did, his expression was as locked down as hers.

When it was time to board, she held out her hand but he coldly ignored it. 'Really?' he said with a cutting edge to his voice.

Emily dropped her hand along with the last of her hopes. Her heart was so heavy it felt as though it were towing the jet she was about to board. Couldn't they at least part as friends? How were they supposed to be parents of their child if they could barely speak to each other? 'I'll let you know the date of the scan.'

'Fine.'

She searched his face for a sign that he was finding this as difficult as she was but there was nothing there. It was as if he had wiped every emotion from the hard drive of his personality. There wasn't even a flicker on the screen of his face. 'Goodbye, Loukas.'

He didn't answer.

Emily turned and walked down the boarding corridor, but when she glanced back for one last look at him he had already gone.

Loukas walked out of the airport before he created a scene. Anger, disappointment and some other nameless emotion were boiling inside him in a toxic mix the like of which he had never quite experienced before. The sense of powerless was overwhelming. He wanted to pick Emily up and carry her fireman-style back to his villa—to give her no choice but to stay with him. He could be ruthless when he needed to be, but her confession of love had stunned him.

Why had she had to throw *that* in the mix? Surely it was just fanciful on her part? Good sex did that to women. To be fair, it did it to men too. But just because the sex was great didn't mean he was in love with her. He had never been in love with anyone. Her confession shouldn't have surprised him so much. She was an affectionate and giving person. Loving came naturally to her. She didn't have to think about it. Guard against it. Block it. It wasn't that he wasn't capable of love. He loved his mother, his sister and his friends but in a remote and hands-off way. Getting close to someone didn't come naturally to him. Maybe it was the way his personality was wired, or maybe it was because of the trauma he'd gone through with his parents' acrimonious divorce and custody battle, not to mention the harrowing guilt he felt over the accident with his sister.

Loving someone scared the hell out of him.

It scared him to be that vulnerable. The odds of losing someone escalated the more you cared about them. The odds of hurting them were even worse.

He remembered how he used to lie in bed at night as a small child listening to his parents argue bitterly. The sense of insecurity had been sickening but he had always comforted himself that no way would his mother ever leave him. His father, yes, but never his mother.

He still remembered the day when his father had taken him roughly by the hand and all but dragged him to the waiting car. Loukas had fought against the tears, not wanting to make it any worse for his distraught mother but, more importantly, not wanting to let his father know how upset he was at leaving his mother behind. His father would have enjoyed that too much. He would have relished in the pain and suffering he was inflicting. Loukas had schooled his features into a mask, just as he had done just now with Emily. But he could still picture his mother running after the car, her hands reaching out to him, her hair flying in disarray about her tear-ravaged face.

Such intense emotion had terrified him then and it terrified him now. He sought refuge in anger because anger was something he could control. He could lock it down and tie it up like a wild animal. He could wait it out. Let it cool off before he looked at it again.

What had Emily been thinking, offering her hand to him like some mild acquaintance? They'd had smoking-hot sex together. They'd made a baby together, for God's sake. How dared she reduce their relationship to an impersonal press of hands at a gate lounge? She had no right to do this when he'd offered her more than he'd offered anyone.

He didn't want to hurt her but how could he pretend to feel things he had never felt for anyone? That was why he had given her the get-out option on their marriage. He had never promised her 'for ever'.

He wasn't that person. He could never be that person.

He wondered now if he ever had been.

CHAPTER NINE

EMILY HAD BEEN back in London a week when the doorbell rang. Her heart leapt as if it were bouncing off a trampoline. Could it be Loukas? Had he changed his mind? Did he love her after all? She had heard nothing from him other than a brief text to make sure she'd got home safely. She had thought about texting him, especially since she couldn't find the little key to the jewellery box, but she didn't want him to think she was using it as an excuse to contact him. The key probably had been lost at the security checkpoint at the airport or when she'd dug out tissue after tissue from her bag on the flight home.

But in a way the box symbolised her despair over Loukas's inability to love her. His heart was as locked as that box. Day after day had gone by and she had watched her phone with bated breath, hoping the next time it rang it would be him. But he never called.

She rushed to the front door of her flat but her heart sank to her feet when she opened it. 'Oh… Mum… I can't talk right now…'

'I just got back from my eight-day yoga retreat and turned on my phone to read your engagement's been called off! What's going on?'

Emily found it hard enough dealing with everyone else's disappointment, let alone her own, so she had only sent the text the day before because she hadn't wanted her mother to counsel her as if she were one of her clients. She had told Allegra about her decision to leave Loukas as soon as she'd got back home and, while Allegra was concerned and sad for her, she knew Loukas well enough to know it was pointless hoping he might change.

She couldn't stop her bottom lip from trembling. 'Oh, Mum. My life is such a terrible mess.'

Her mother stepped inside and closed the door then, after a brief hesitation, held her arms out. 'Tell me everything.'

Emily stepped into her mother's hug that for some reason didn't feel as stiff and awkward as normal. She sobbed her way through the story of the last few days. 'He was only offering to marry me out of a sense of duty. But I love him. How could I marry him, knowing he doesn't love me back?'

Her mother patted her back and made soothing, cooing noises as though she were settling a fractious baby. 'You can't. You did the right thing in putting an end to it.'

They moved to sit together on the sofa and her mother kept handing her a steady supply of tissues. 'It'll be okay, poppet. You'll get through it.'

'But I'm so unhappy!'

'I know, I felt like that when I broke up with my fiancé. I literally wanted to die.'

Emily lifted her head out of her hands to stare at her mother. 'Your fiancé? When were you engaged?'

Her mother gave her a sad, twisted little smile. 'It was a couple of months before I went to the music festival. His name was Mark. We were madly, passionately in love—or at least, I was. He clearly wasn't. We were getting married but then he broke it off a week before the wedding. He married another girl a few weeks later. She was from money—heaps of money. I didn't take it well. I kind of…lost myself there for a while.'

She let out a long sigh. 'Drugs, sex, rock and roll—you name it. But then, getting pregnant with you turned my life around. Sort of.' She squeezed

Emily's hand. 'I know I'm not the best mother in the world. But after Mark broke my heart I couldn't settle to anything for long. I lived with a constant fear of it being snatched away from me. So I became the one who moved on before someone could do that to me again. I even kept you at arm's length because I was frightened I might lose you too.'

'Oh, Mum.' Emily hugged her mother close. 'I had no idea. Why didn't you tell me about him before now?'

Her mother eased back to look at her. 'I was ashamed of being such a naïve fool over him. How could I have not known he was not as invested in the relationship as me? One minute we were planning the wedding, and then the next I was calling everyone to say it was off. It was the most embarrassing thing, having to hand back all those presents. For years I only had to look at a wedding dress and I'd want to throw up. It infuriated me that I hadn't seen what was right before my eyes. That's why I was so worried about you and Daniel. I could sense he wasn't the one for you. I want you to be happy. I want you to have the "for ever" love I can't seem to find no matter how hard I try.'

Emily frowned. 'But I thought you were happy with your footloose and fancy-free lifestyle?'

Her mother let out a puff of air. 'Why do you

think I teach all this couples' intimacy stuff? Because I'm rubbish at it in my personal life.'

Emily's shoulders drooped. 'Yeah, well, it seems I'm not too great at it, either.'

'So the sex wasn't good?'

She couldn't believe she was discussing her sex life with her mother. 'No, it was amazing. It was the one thing we were good at—better than good. Perfect.'

Her mother shifted her lips from side to side in a thoughtful manner. 'If only I'd met him and seen him with you I could have told you for sure if he was the one for you. Body language doesn't lie.'

'I already know he's the one for me,' Emily said, taking another tissue and sighing deeply. 'Thing is, he doesn't think he's the right one for anyone.'

Six weeks later...

Loukas was glad his work called him away to the States for a few weeks because he was sick to death of his housekeeper casting him How-could-you-have-let-her-go? looks that grated on his nerves like a file on a bad tooth. He was doing his best not to think about Emily so he didn't appreciate Chrysanthe reminding him at every opportunity that he hadn't gone after her.

What would have been the point? She had made up her mind. He would only be lying to her if he got her back by telling her what she wanted to hear. That was the sort of thing his father would do. She had made her decision and he had to respect it. At least she was allowing him access to his child, but it stung a little that he wasn't there twenty-four-seven so he could see the changes in her body as the baby grew. Was she still nauseous? Did she still feel faint? What if she was sick and needed help? Who would she call? She didn't seem all that close to her mother, in spite of her words to the contrary.

He had thought about calling or texting but he hadn't trusted himself not to plead with her to come back. He wasn't the sort of man to beg. That was a lesson he'd learned a long time ago. He'd once begged his father to take him back to his mother. He'd been sent to his room and only allowed out once he'd apologised for being ungrateful. He had stayed in his room for two weeks, only coming out for meals and bathroom visits. His begging had given his father even more power over him and he had sworn he would never allow anyone to do that to him again.

But it wasn't just his housekeeper on his back. Draco and Allegra had been at him as well. He'd told them to back off. He was in London to see

Emily at the twelve-week scan today, and that was all he was prepared to do in terms of contact before the scan. The press had noted he and Emily were currently living apart, but apparently they had other much more scandalous couples to follow now, and had left both of them alone.

The only people who hadn't said anything to him were his mother and sister. A month ago that wouldn't have been all that unusual. Sometimes several months went by without any contact from them. But, since they knew of Emily's pregnancy and his intention to marry her, why hadn't they contacted him and offered commiserations at the very least? It said a lot about his relationship with them. They were as distant with him as he was with them.

Or was it because Ariana was disappointed she wasn't going to be a bridesmaid after all? His sister's one chance of being part of a bridal party and he had ruined it. Or maybe they had sided with Emily since they had met her and seen her warm and generous personality for themselves.

He could hardly blame them for shifting loyalties. How could they not prefer her to him? She was all he was not. She was love, laughter and hope while he was an emotionless wasteland. They would probably think she'd had a lucky escape from a loveless union with him.

But would it have been loveless?

The thought kept at him, catching him off-guard at odd moments. He already loved his child even though it was still only a tiny foetus. He'd been on that pregnancy website every day. It was almost like an obsession now. First thing in the morning—if he had even been to sleep, that was—he would check it out. He'd even been on a baby-name site, trawling through names, wondering whether his baby was a girl or boy. He had even been checking out baby wear and toy shops. He'd bought a hand-made teddy bear while he'd been in New York and, when the shop assistant had asked him if it was for his child, he'd been ridiculously proud to say yes.

But along with that pride was a niggling sense of disappointment Emily hadn't been with him to help him choose it. Weren't they supposed to be doing this together? Wasn't that part of the joy of welcoming a child into the world? Preparing the nursery, buying a pram and car seat, a high chair and a cot? How was he supposed to do it without her? What was the point of anything without her?

Loukas didn't like admitting it but he missed her. He missed her smile with its adorable dimples, her cute little rabbit-twitch, her soft hands and how it felt when they touched him. He couldn't imagine making love with anyone else. The thought hadn't even crossed his mind.

He only wanted her.

His gaze drifted to the tiny gold key on his hotel room's desk. He had found it on the floor by the bed after Emily had left. She must have dropped it when she stuffed the jewellery box in her handbag. She'd thought he hadn't noticed but he'd seen her in the reflection of the mirror. He couldn't understand why she had bothered taking it. He picked up the key and turned it over a couple of times. It had cost more than the silly little box. Way more. Why had she left the most expensive gifts and taken that old box that wasn't even worth the money he'd paid for it?

He put the key back on his desk, but every few minutes his gaze would go back to it. She couldn't open the box without the key and the key was useless to him without the box. He suddenly realised Emily was like that tiny, golden key. She had come into his life and picked the lock on his heart. He'd thought it was lust that had driven him to seek her out, but now he wondered if something else had been going on. Something he had never encountered before. Something that dismantled all the barriers he'd put up over the years.

It was easy to lust after someone. It took no

courage at all. But loving someone was different. It opened you up to hurt, to vulnerability.

But it also opened you up to healing.

Loukas had never considered himself a coward. He had prided himself he'd always faced up to responsibility and never shirked from a task because it was unpleasant or inconvenient. But hadn't he been hiding away from love? Lacking the courage to explore the emotions he had locked down deep inside him?

Emily had found the key to him. Her bright, cheery smile had shone on all the dark, shuttered and shadowed places in his soul, illuminating him with a beam of hope for the first time in years.

His professional reputation was built on his ability to keep places, people and top level security systems secure, and yet a cute little clumsy Englishwoman had stumbled into his life and cracked his code.

He *loved* her.

Wasn't that why he had sought her out in London a month after Draco and Allegra's wedding? He hadn't been able to get her out of his mind. But it wasn't just his mind that was captivated by her.

It was his heart.

Loukas had a couple of hours until he met with her at the hospital for the scan. Should he wait till then or go and see her now? How could he wait two minutes, let alone two hours?

He could and he would, because there were things he had to do before then so that she would be absolutely convinced he loved her.

Emily had a full bladder and an empty heart when she arrived at the hospital for the scan. Her mother had offered to come with her but Emily had decided against it. She didn't trust her mother not to give Loukas an earful about his 'love' issues. Emily had texted him the time and place and he'd responded with a curt 'Thanks'. It seemed so impersonal and clinical; nothing like she expected it would be when having a child with someone she loved. She placed a hand over her abdomen. She had ballooned over the last week. Not a party balloon, either. A hot-air balloon. Surely it wasn't normal to show this much so soon? She could barely do up the top button on her cotton trousers. Or maybe it was nerves. Maybe it wasn't butterflies in her stomach but bats—big spiky-winged ones, beating around in there in panic at the thought of seeing Loukas again.

Oh, God, why had she said he could come to the scan? Maybe she should've just sent him the photo. No. That wouldn't be fair. He was the baby's father. He had a right to be here if he wanted to be.

A nurse directed her to the cubicle to wait for the sonographer. 'Is anyone going to be with you?'

'My…erm…the baby's father said he'd be here.' Emily glanced out at the reception and waiting room area but there was no sign yet of Loukas. Surely he would turn up? Or had he changed his mind? He hated hospitals, but surely he wouldn't let that get in the way of seeing his child for the first time?

'No problem,' the nurse said. 'We'll get you set up and then when he arrives I'll send him in.'

Emily lay on the table and waited with her hands over her rounded belly. She hoped Loukas wouldn't be too long otherwise her bladder was going to have something to say about it. Where was he? She'd told him the right time. Surely he wouldn't let her down on this day of all days?

The plastic clock on the wall mechanically clicked its seconds. Tick. Tick. Tick.

Laughter came from the reception area and the sound of someone squealing with delight. 'Oh, how cute are you two little darlings?'

Emily assumed a mother had come in with a toddler or two. She wondered if the mum had a partner, someone who loved her as much as she loved him. She tried not to cry, but her emotions were on shaky ground as it was. This wasn't the way she'd thought it would be. She'd pictured this day when she was younger, imagining how exciting it would be to be holding hands with her partner as they met their tiny baby *in utero*. Now she was a frazzled mess of nerves because the only partner she wanted didn't love her. He liked her. He desired her. But he didn't love her. Why wasn't he here? Had he got more important things to do than meet his baby for the first time?

The curtain was suddenly swished back and Loukas came in. The cubicle had seemed spacious until he entered it. Or maybe that was because, this close to him, she ached to reach out and touch him. She curled her fingers into her palms to stop herself. She could smell the fresh citrus scent of him and longed for him to lean down and press a kiss to her mouth. 'Sorry I'm late,' he said. 'I got held up with…something.'

'Work?' She couldn't quite remove the barb in her tone in time.

His expression registered her comment with a tiny flinch near the edge of his mouth. She noted he had cut himself shaving for he had a little scratch on his cheek. But then she noticed he had two or three scratches on his hands as well.

'How are you?' He swallowed and glanced at her bulging tummy. 'Growing by the minute, by the look of things.'

'Yes, well, some of that may well be my bladder,' Emily said. 'If you make me laugh then things could get pretty awkward around here.' Not that he was likely to make her laugh any time soon. All she wanted to do was cry.

'How's the nausea?'

'A little better.'

'That's good.'

God, how stiff and formal they sounded! Like two people who had only just met and were making idle chit-chat to fill in the time. 'So, how are your mum and sister?' Emily asked. 'Have you seen them lately?'

'I haven't seen them but I spoke to them an hour ago. I thought you might like to visit them with me after this.'

She frowned. 'Why would I do that?'

The sonographer came in just then and began setting up the ultrasound equipment. A generous layer of gel was smeared over Emily's belly and the sonographer angled the screen so both Emily and Loukas could see. 'So, here we have the placental sac... Hang on a minute.' She fiddled with the dials on the machine for a few moments, a frown of concentration pulling at her forehead.

Emily's heart pounded as though she had just bolted up ten flights of stairs. What was wrong?

Why was the sonographer peering at the screen so intently? She glanced at Loukas. He too was frowning and his hand suddenly reached for hers and squeezed it. 'What's wrong?' he asked.

The sonographer turned on her stool and smiled at them both. 'Have a look.' She pointed to the screen with the cursor. 'Here is your baby's heartbeat. See that? And here is another one.'

Another heartbeat?

Emily met Loukas's stunned gaze. 'Twins?' he asked.

'We're having *twins*?' Emily echoed him.

'You are indeed having twins,' the sonographer said. 'And they're identical, from what I can see. Congratulations. I'll print out the pictures for you while you sit here and get acquainted with your babies for a while. I won't be long.' The curtain swished closed.

Emily couldn't stop staring at the screen where their babies were curled up like two peanuts. 'Oh. My. God.'

Loukas brought her hand up to his mouth and kissed it. His eyes were moist and he seemed to be having trouble speaking. He opened and closed his mouth a couple of times but didn't get any words out.

'I'm sorry,' Emily said, her bottom lip beginning to tremble. 'Trust me to not do anything by halves. You didn't even want one baby and now I've given you two.'

'No, don't say that,' he said when he was finally able to speak. 'I do want the baby—I mean, babies. I want you too. I love you, Emily. So, so much.'

Emily wasn't sure if she should believe him. He had just been informed they were having twins. He might be able to let her walk away from him with one baby, but two was something else again. If he was so sure he loved her, why wait until today? Why not some time over the last six weeks? She narrowed her gaze. 'How do I know you're not just saying that because we're having twins?'

He held her hand against his chest where she could feel the thud of his heart. She was no cardiac doctor but it seemed to be racing as hard and fast as hers. 'I only realised it a couple of hours ago. I know how unlikely that sounds—I should have realised the moment I met you that you were the only woman for me. I'm sorry for putting you through hell these last weeks, but I've been a coward. I didn't want to fall in love because everyone I've loved in the past I've hurt. I convinced myself I hadn't fallen for you, but I think I did at Draco and Allegra's wedding when you caught the bouquet and smiled at me with those gorgeous dimples of yours showing.'

Emily wanted to believe him but she had been so hurt by his distance these last few weeks. 'I don't know…it seems a little too convenient to me.'

'I can prove it, *agape mou*,' he said. 'I have a surprise waiting for you in the waiting room. The reception staff are minding them for me. That's what all that laughter you can hear is about. I bought you a present to convince you I love you and want to spend the rest of my life with you.'

'You buy presents for everyone,' Emily said with a little scowl. 'It doesn't mean you love them.'

'I know, and that's been my mistake in the past,' he said. 'But when you took everything but the jewellery box key I realised how much I loved you. You're my key. You've unlocked my heart and wriggled your way into my life to such a degree I can't bear to be without you.'

'I wondered where that key went,' Emily said. 'I haven't been able to open the box. I locked it after I took the earrings out before I left your place. I tried picking the lock with a nail file but it didn't work.' But despite Loukas's words she still wasn't convinced he was truly in love with her and she kept frowning at him.

'Will you at least come with me to visit Ariana and my mother once we're done here?' Loukas asked. 'I have a present for Ariana as well as you. Please? Will you just come and see, and then you'll know I'm not lying?'

Emily climbed off the bed with his help. 'Maybe I should go to the bathroom first.'

'Good idea.'

When she came out of the bathroom, Loukas took her by the hand and smiled down at her. 'Ready?'

Emily walked with him to the reception area to find two adorable Irish Retriever puppies being babysat by the reception staff. She promptly burst into tears and turned blindly into Loukas's chest, hugging him tightly. 'I can't believe you bought me a dog. Two dogs! Are you even allowed to bring them in here?'

He smiled down at her tear-stained face. 'I told the staff they're therapy dogs. One is for Ariana. It will give us a good excuse to visit for play dates. Will you help me build my relationship with my mother and sister? They already love you and can't wait to see you.'

Emily leaned back to gaze up at him. 'You really do love me, don't you?'

His eyes were glistening with moisture. 'I love you more than I can say. Will you marry me, my precious love? Will you be my wife and help me raise our family?'

She touched his face as if to see if he was really standing there in front of her. Not just in front of her, but all the patients and staff as well, who were watching with avid interest, faces beaming. 'I will marry you. I love you. I can't wait to spend the rest of my life with you. I've been so lonely and sad without you these past weeks.'

He held her close. 'Me too. What a fool I've been for waiting so long to tell you. And then, when I did tell you, you didn't believe me. That was a bad moment.'

'But saved by those adorable little puppies,' she said, slipping out of his arms to go to cuddle them and having her face thoroughly licked in the process. 'Do they have names?'

'Not yet, we have to choose them. While we're at it we'd better get working on our babies' ones as well.'

Emily handed him one puppy to hold while she cuddled the other. 'You've made me so happy, darling. I feel like pinching myself to make sure I'm not dreaming this.'

Loukas stretched his neck to avoid a wet puppy tongue aiming for his chin. 'Forget about pinching yourself. These little guys have needle-sharp teeth that will more than do the job for you.'

Emily laughed. 'And here I was, thinking you'd cut yourself shaving. Although, I did wonder how you scratched your hands.'

Loukas grinned. 'I'm dying to kiss you but I'm worried it might turn into a foursome if I bend down while we're holding these little rascals.'

'Kiss her. Kiss her!' the reception staff and patients chanted.

Loukas's eyes twinkled. 'Are you up for it?'

Emily lifted her face to his. 'You bet.'

EPILOGUE

Loukas stood at the end of the aisle at the St Sypridion Church on Corfu. He could barely see through the blur of moisture in his eyes when he saw Ariana coming down the aisle in her chair behind Allegra. It had only been a couple of weeks but already his relationship with his sister and mother was in a better place. A good place. A place where they could talk about the accident and how it had impacted on all of them. His mother had even confessed her own crushing guilt over not watching Ariana in that split moment when she'd gone off to ride her bike. Because he had been so focussed on his own guilt, he hadn't realised his mother had been in her own private hell for all these years.

But seeing Ariana now, filled with joy for him, he felt a sense of peace she too one day would find the love and happiness he had found with Emily.

He looked at his mother, who was in the front

row, mopping tears from her eyes, and another wave of emotion rolled through him. She smiled and gave him a little wave and he smiled back, full of love and admiration for her, for how she had supported his sister and now welcomed Emily to the family as if she were her own daughter.

Emily's mother was in the front row on the bride's side and she winked cheekily at him. He genuinely liked Willow, especially since he'd passed the Body Language Intimacy test, whatever the hell that was. Not that he needed anyone's approval, other than his beloved Emily's, but it was nice to know her mother was part of his family now.

And then, just when he thought he had his emotions back under control, in came Emily. Nothing could have prepared him for that moment. She was dressed in a beautiful French lace dress that couldn't quite hide the swell of her belly where their twin babies were continuing to thrive. She was glowing with good health and radiant with love. The same love he could feel beaming out of him as she took her place by his side. He took her hands and gave them a gentle squeeze. 'You look so beautiful, you took my breath away.'

Her dimples appeared when she smiled. 'Didn't Ariana look amazing?'

His heart gave a spasm of happiness. 'You've given me back my family, *agape mou*.'

She leaned a little closer to whisper. 'Speaking of families. Allegra has some news.'

Loukas glanced at Allegra but she was looking dreamily at Draco, one of her hands pressing against her abdomen underneath the bouquet she was holding. Loukas smiled at Emily. 'Looks like we're not the only ones starting a family.'

'I know. Isn't it exciting?'

'Ready?' the priest asked, stepping forward to begin the service.

'Are we?' Loukas asked, winking at Emily.

Her sparkling brown eyes twinkled back. 'We're ready.'

* * * * *

Get 2 Free Books,
Plus 2 Free Gifts—
just for trying the Reader Service!

*Natasha Pellegrini and Matteo Manaserro's reunion
catches them both in a potent mix of emotion, and they
surrender to their explosive passion. Natasha was a
virgin until Matteo's touch branded her as his and
when Matteo discovers Natasha is pregnant,
he's intent on claiming his baby. Except he hasn't
bargained on their insatiable chemistry binding them
together so completely!*

Read on for a sneak preview of
Michelle Smart's *book*
CLAIMING HIS ONE-NIGHT BABY,
the second part of her
BOUND TO A BILLIONAIRE *trilogy.*

"Come to Miami with me. I'm flying to Caballeros with
Daniele tomorrow. We should be there for only a couple of
days. When I get back I'll take you home with me. We can
say you need a break from everything. In a month or so we
can tell them you're pregnant with my child. It'll be easier
for them to accept we turned to each other for comfort and
that a relationship grew naturally than to accept the truth of
the child's conception."

"You want us to lie?"

"No, I do not want us to lie. I despise dishonesty but
what's the alternative? Do you want to return to your parents
in England and…"

"No." Her rebuttal was emphatic.

"Then coming with me is the only answer. If you stay in Pisa, and Vanessa and the others think there is even a chance you are carrying Pieta's... To build their hopes up only to cut them away would be too cruel. We need to show a united front starting from now."

"So you do accept the baby's yours?"

"Yes. I accept it's mine and I will acknowledge it as mine. Come with me and I will protect you both, and we will have a small chance of making the pain of what's to come a little less in the family who has shown both of us nothing but love and acceptance. They have suffered enough."

She rested her head against the window and closed her eyes. He hated that even looking as if she hadn't slept in a month she was still the most beautiful woman he'd ever laid eyes on.

Eventually she nodded. "Okay," she said in her soft, clear voice. "I'll come to Miami with you. But only for a while. We can fake a burgeoning relationship, I can get pregnant and then we can split up."

"We stay together until it's born."

Her eyes flew open to stare at him with incredulity. "That's seven and a half months away."

Don't miss
CLAIMING HIS ONE-NIGHT BABY,
available September 2017 wherever
Harlequin Presents® books and ebooks are sold.

www.Harlequin.com

HPEXP082017R